LIN

BY WALTER CRANE

PREFACE

As in the case of "The Bases of Design," to which this is intended to form a companion volume, the substance of the following chapters on Line and Form originally formed a series of lectures delivered to the students of the Manchester Municipal School of Art.

There is no pretension to an exhaustive treatment of a subject it would be difficult enough to exhaust, and it is dealt with in a way intended to bear rather upon the practical work of an art school, and to be suggestive and helpful to those face to face with the current problems of drawing and design.

These have been approached from a personal point of view, as the results of conclusions arrived at in the course of a busy working life which has left but few intervals for the elaboration of theories apart from practice, and such as they are, these papers are now offered to the wider circle of students and workers in the arts of design as from one of themselves.

They were illustrated largely by means of rough sketching in line before my student audience, as well as by photographs and drawings. The rough diagrams have been re-drawn, and the other illustrations reproduced, so that both line and tone blocks are used, uniformity being sacrificed to fidelity.

WALTER CRANE.

Kensington, *July*, 1900.

[vi]

CHAPTER I

Origin and Function of Outline—Silhouette—Definition of Boundaries by—Power of Characterization by—Formation of Letters—Methods of Drawing in Line—The Progressive Method—The Calligraphic Method—The Tentative Method—The Japanese Direct Brush Method—The Oval Method—The Rectangular Method—Quality of Line—Linear Expression of Movement—Textures—Emotion—Scale of Linear Expression.

OUTLINE, one might say, is the Alpha and Omega of Art. It is the earliest mode of expression among primitive peoples, as it is with the individual child, and it has been cultivated for its power of characterization and expression, and as an ultimate test of draughtsmanship, by the most accomplished artists of all time.

The old fanciful story of its origin in the work of a lover who traced in charcoal the boundary of the shadow of the head of his sweetheart as cast upon the wall by the sun, and thus obtained the first profile portrait, is probably more true in substance than in fact, but it certainly illustrates the *function* of outline as the definition of the boundaries of form.

Silhouette[2]

As children we probably perceive forms in nature defined as flat shapes of colour relieved upon other colours, or flat fields of light on dark, as a white horse is defined upon the green grass of a field, or a black figure upon a background of snow.

Definition of Boundaries

To define the boundaries of such forms becomes the main object in early attempts at artistic expression. The attention is caught by the edges—the shape of the silhouette which remains the paramount means of distinction of form when details and secondary [3]characteristics are lost; as the outlines of mountains remain, or are even more clearly seen, when distance subdues the details of their structure, and evening mists throw them into flat planes one behind the other, and leave nothing but the delicate lines of their edges to tell their character. We feel the beauty and simplicity of such effects in nature. We feel that the mind, through the eye resting upon these quiet planes and delicate lines, receives a sense of repose and poetic suggestion which is lost in the bright noontide, with all its wealth of glittering detail, sharp cut in light and shade. There is no doubt that this typical power of outline and the value of simplicity of mass were perceived by the ancients, notably the Ancient Egyptians and the Greeks, who both, in their own ways, in their art show a wonderful power of characterization by means of line and mass, and a delicate sense of the ornamental value and quality of line.

Formation of Letters[4]

Regarding line—the use of outline from the point of view of its value as a means of definition of form and fact—its power is really only limited by the power of draughtsmanship at the command of the artist. From the archaic potters' primitive figures or the rudimentary attempts of children at human or animal forms up to the most refined outlines of a Greek vase-painter, or say the artist of the Dream of Poliphilus, the difference is one of degree. The tyro with the pen, learning to write, splotches and scratches, and painfully forms trembling, limping O's and A's, till with practice and habitude, almost unconsciously, the power to form firm letters is acquired.

Writing, after all, is but a simpler form of drawing, and we know that the letters of our alphabet were originally pictures or symbols. The main difference is that writing stops short with the acquisition of the purely useful power of forming letters and words, and is seldom pursued for the sake of its beauty or artistic qualities as formerly; while drawing continually leads on to new difficulties to be conquered, to new subtleties of line, and fresh fascinations in the pursuit of distinction and style.

The practice of forming letters with the pen or brush, from good types, Roman and Gothic, however, would afford very good preliminary practice to a student of line and form. The hand would acquire directness of stroke and touch, while the eye would grow accustomed to good lines of composition and simple constructive forms. The progressive nature of writing—the gradual building up of the forms of the letters—and the necessity of [5]dealing with recurring forms and lines, also, would bear usefully upon after work in actual design. Albert Dürer in his "Geometrica" gives methods on which to draw the Roman capitals, and also the black letters, building the former upon the square and its proportions, the thickness of the down strokes being one-eighth of square, the thin strokes [6]being one-sixteenth, and the serifs being turned by circles of one-fourth and one-eighth diameter. The capital O, it will be noted, is formed of two circles struck diagonally.

Methods of Drawing in Line

Letters may be taken as the simplest form of definition by means of line. They have been reduced through centuries of use from their primitive hieroglyphic forms to their present arbitrary and fixed types, though even these fixed types are subject to the variation produced by changes of taste and fancy.

But when we come to unformulated nature—to the vast world of complex forms, ever changing their aspect, full of life and movement, trees, flowers, woods and waters, birds, beasts, fishes, the human form—the problem how to represent any of these forms, to express and characterize them by means of so abstract a method as line-drawing, seems at first difficult enough.

But since the growth of perception, like the power of graphic representation, is gradual and partial, though progressive, the eye and the mind are generally first impressed with the salient features and leading characteristics of natural forms, just as the child's first idea of a human form is that of a body with four straight limbs, with a preponderating head. That is the first impression, and it is unhesitatingly recorded in infantine outline.

The first aim, then, in drawing anything in line is to grasp the general truths of form, character, and expression.

The Progressive Method

There are various methods of proceeding in getting an outline of any object or figure. To begin with, the student might begin progressively defining [7]the form by a series of stages in this way. Take the profile of a bird, for instance; the form might be gradually built up by the combination of a series of lines:

or take the simpler form of a flask bottle:

or a jar on the same principle:

or, simpler still, a leaf form, putting in the stem first with one stroke (1):

and building the form around it (2, 3).

The Calligraphic Method

This might be termed the calligraphic method of drawing; and in this method facility of hand might be further practised by attempting the definition of forms by continuous strokes, or building it up by [8]as few strokes as possible. The simpler types of ornament consisting of meandering and flowing lines can all be produced in this way, i.e., by continuous line, as well as natural forms treated in a [9]certain abstract or conventional way, which adapts them to decoration.

The Tentative Method

Another method is to sketch in lightly guide lines for main masses, building a sort of scaffolding of light lines to assist the eye in getting the correct outline in its place, using vertical centre lines for symmetrical forms to get the poise right.[10]This is the method very generally in use, but I think it very desirable to practise direct drawing as well, to acquire certainty of eye and facility of hand; and one must not mind failure at first, as this kind of power and facility is so much a matter of practice.

The Japanese Direct Brush Method

The Japanese, who draw with the brush, have accustomed themselves to draw in a direct manner without any preliminary sketching, and the charm of their work is largely owing to that crisp freshness of touch only possible to their direct method. The great object is to establish a perfectly intimate correspondence between eye and hand, so that the latter will record what the former perceives.

Abundant specimens of the freedom and naturalism of the modern school of Japanese artists in this direct brush method may be found in the work of Bari, Hiroshigi, and Hokusai, and in the numerous prints and books of designs from their hands. To all draughtsmen and designers they are most valuable to study for their direct method and simple means of expression of form and fact. Accidental as they frequently seem in composition, the placing of the drawing upon the paper is carefully considered before starting, and this, of course, is always a very important point.

Yet another method of drawing, more especially in relation to the drawing of the human figure and animal forms, I may mention as a help to those who do not feel strong enough for the direct method. At the same time it must be borne in mind that we can accustom ourselves to *any* method; and the more dependent we become upon a single [11]method, the less facility we shall have for working in any other. But for all that it is desirable to master *one* method—that is, to be able to draw in line *freely* in one way or another—and experience and practice alone will enable us to find the method most satisfactory.

The Oval and Rectangular Methods

The Rectangular Method

This other method is to block in the principal [12]masses of the forms we desire to represent by means of a series of ovals, as shown in the illustration, and when we have got the masses in their proper relations, to proceed to draw in the careful outline of the figure, or whatever it may be, upon this substructure of guiding lines, correcting as we go along. It would be quite possible to work on the same principle, but upon a structure of more or less rectangular masses. The real use of the method is to assist the student to get a grasp of the relation of the masses of a figure and a sense of structure in drawing; whether square or oval blocking in is used may be a matter of choice. It may be said for the oval forms that they resemble the contours of the structure in human and animal forms.

If one had a tendency to round one's forms too much, it would be well to try the rectangular method to correct this, and *vice versâ*.

After a certain facility has been acquired in rendering form by means of line, we shall perceive further capacities of expression in its use, and begin to note how different characteristics of form and natural fact may be expressed by varying the quality of our outline.

If we are drawing a plant or a flower, for instance, we should endeavour to show by the quality of our line the difference between the fine springing curves in the structure of the lily, the solid seed-centre and stiff radiation of the petals of the daisy, and the delicate silky folds of the poppy.

Quality of Line

But, as leaves come before flowers, it would be best to begin with leaf forms and try to express the character of oak and beech, lime and chestnut [13]leaves, for instance, by means of outline. Probably at first we shall feel dissatisfied with our outline as not being full enough: it may look meagre in quality and small in definition of form. This [14]probably arises from not allowing enough space—from setting the outline too much within the boundary of the form. To correct this one cannot do better than block in the form of the object we are drawing (leaf, flower, or figure) with a full brush in black silhouette, placing the object against the light or white paper, so that its true boundary may be seen uninterfered with by surface markings or shadows, and, concentrating our attention upon the *edge*, follow it as carefully as possible with the solid black. Then, if we compare the result with our outline, it will help to show where it has failed; and the practice of thus blocking in with the brush in solid silhouette will tend to encourage a larger style of drawing, since good outline means good perception of mass; and as a general principle in drawing, it may be recommended to place one's [15]outline*outside* the silhouette boundary of the form rather than within it; that is to say, when the figure or object is relieved in light against dark, as the line in that case defines the edge against the background. When the figure or object appears as dark upon a light ground, however, the outline should be within the silhouette, obviously, or its delicate boundary is lost.

Linear Expression of Movement

Another important attribute of line is its power of expressing or suggesting *movement*. By a law of inseparable association, undulating lines approaching the horizontal, or leading down to it, are connected with the sense of repose; whereas broken curves and rectangular lines always suggest action and unrest, or the resistance to force of some kind.

The recurrence of a series of lines in the same direction in a kind of crescendo or wave-like movement suggests continuous pressure of force in the same direction, as in this series of instantaneous actions of a man bowling, where the line drawn through or touching the highest points in [16]each figure takes the line of the curve of a wave. The wave-line, indeed, may be said not only to suggest movement, but also to describe its direction and force. It is, in fact, *the line of movement*. The principle may be seen in a simpler way, as Hogarth points out in his "Analysis of Beauty," by observing the line described along a wall by the head of a man walking along the street. Or, as we may see sometimes near the coast, trees exposed to the constant pressure of the wind illustrate this recurrence of lines in the same direction governing their general shape; and as each tree is forced to spread in the direction away from the wind, the effect is that of their being always struggling against its pressure even in the calmest weather; and this is entirely due to our association of wind-movement with this peculiar linear expression.

Flowing water, again, is expressed by certain recurring wave-lines, which remind us of the ancient linear symbols of the zigzag and meander used from the earliest times to express water. In the [17]streams that channel the sands of the sea-shore when the tide recedes we may see beautiful flowing lines, sometimes crossing like a network, and sometimes running into a series of shell-like waves; while the sands themselves are ribbed and channelled and modelled by the recurring movement [18]of the waves, which leave upon them the impress and the expression of their motion (much as in a more delicate medium the air-currents impress the fields of cloud, and give them their characteristic forms).

Linear Expression of Textures

Textures and surfaces, too, fall within the range of linear expression. One would naturally use lines of totally different consistency and character to express rough or smooth surfaces: to express the difference of value, for instance, between the ivory-like smoothness of an egg and the scaly surface of a pine-cone, entirely different qualities of line are obviously wanted. The firm-set yet soft feathers of the plumage of a bird must be rendered by a very different touch from the shining scales of a fish. The hair and horns of animals, delicate human features, flowers, the sinuous lines of thin drapery, or the broad massive folds of heavy robes, all demand from the designer and draughtsman in line different kinds of suggestive expression, a translation or rendering of natural fact subordinate to the artistic purpose of his work, and in relation to the material and purpose for which he works.

Linear Expression of Emotion

Then, again, when we come to the expression of ideas—of thought and sentiment—we find in line an abstract but direct medium for their illustration; and this again, too, by means of that law of inseparable association which connects the idea of praise or aspiration and ascension, for instance, with long lines inclining towards the severe vertical, as when we draw a figure with upraised hands; while the feeling might be increased if led up to or re-echoed by other groups and objects in the [19]composition, forming a kind of vertical crescendo on the same principle which we were considering in regard to the expression of lateral movement. Few things in design are finer or more elevated in feeling than William Blake's design of the Morning Stars singing together, in the series of the Book [20]of Job, yet it is little more than a vertical arrangement of figures with uplifted and intercrossing arms. The linear plan gives the main impetus to the expressiveness of the design, and is the basis [21]of the beauty, which culminates in the rapture of the fresh youthful faces.

Scale of Linear Expression

Bowed and bent lines tending downwards, on the other hand, convey the opposite ideas of dejection and despair. This is illustrated in these figures of Flaxman's, who was a great master of style in outline.

Capacity of Line

We seem here to discover a kind of scale of linear expression—the two extremes at either end: the horizontal and the vertical, with every degree and modulation between them; the undulating curve giving way to the springing energetic spiral, the meandering, flowing line sinking to the horizontal: or the sharp opposition and thrust of rectangular, the nervous resistance of broken curves, the flame-like, triumphant, ascending verticals. Truly the designer may find a great range of expression within the dominion of pure line. Line is, indeed, as I have before termed it, a [22]language, a most sensitive and vigorous speech of many dialects; which can adapt itself to all purposes, and is, indeed, indispensable to all the provinces of design in line. Line may be regarded simply as a means of record, a method of registering the facts of nature, of graphically portraying the characteristics of plants and animals, or the features of humanity: the smooth features of youth, the rugged lines of age. It is capable of this, and more also, since it can appeal to our emotions and evoke our passionate and poetic sympathies with both the life of humanity and wild nature, as in the hands of the great masters it lifts us to the heavens or bows us down to earth: we may stand on the sea-shore and see the movement of the falling waves, the fierce energy of the storm and its rolling armament of clouds, glittering with the sudden zigzag of the lightning; or we may sink into the profound calm of a summer day, when the mountains, defined only by their edges, wrapped in soft planes of mist, seem to recline upon the level meadows like Titans and dream of the golden age.

[23]

CHAPTER II

The Language of Line—Dialects—Comparison of the Style of various Artists in Line—Scale of Degrees in Line—Picture Writing—Relation of Line to Form—Two Paths—The Graphic Purpose—Aspect—The Ornamental Purpose—Typical Treatment or Convention—Rhythm—Linear Plans in Pattern Designing—Wall-paper Design—Controlling Forms—Memory—Evolution in Design—Variety in Unity—Counterbalance—Linear Logic—Recurring Line and Form—Principle of Radiation—Range and Use of Line.

I SPOKE of Line as a Language, and gave some illustrations of its power and range of expression, showing that line is capable not only of recording natural fact and defining character, but also of conveying the idea of movement and force, of action and repose; and, further, of appealing to our emotions and thoughts by variations and changes in its direction, the degree of its emphasis, and other qualities.

Dialects

Yet every designer and draughtsman uses line in a different way, and of a different quality, according to his preference, habit, training, or personality. The endless variations which result I should—to pursue the analogy of speech further—term *dialects.* We might collect abundant examples of these from the work of line-designers since the world began, or compare the methods of any of the popular illustrators of to-day to find constant[24]variations and individual differences occurring even among those which might be said, under the influence of a prevailing mode, to be variations of one type.

Compare a Greek vase-painter's delicate brush line-drawing with the bold pen-line of Albert Dürer (to get a contrast in historic style). Compare (to take two masters of different schools, but of the same country) the line-treatment of Mantegna with the line-treatment of Raphael; or, to take another jump, compare the line-work of Blake and Flaxman; or, to take a modern instance, and to come to our own contemporary artists, compare a drawing by Burne-Jones and one by Phil May.

We might construct a sort of scale of the degrees and qualities of line.

There is, for instance, outline of every degree of boldness or fineness, from the strong black half-inch outline and upwards used in mosaic-work and stained-glass leading; the outline of the pattern designer for block-printing; the outline of the pen draughtsman for process-work or woodcut; and so on, down to the hair-line of the drypoint etcher.

Scale of Degrees in Line

There are the *qualities* of line in different degrees of firmness, roughness, raggedness, or smooth and flowing. There are the degrees of *direction* of line, curvilinear or angular. On the angular side all variations from the perpendicular and horizontal, or rectangle, within which we may find all these degrees, and on the curvilinear side, all the variations from spiral to circle: so that we might say that the rectangle was the cradle of all[25]angular variations of line, while the semicircle was the cradle of all curvilinear variations. (See the diagrams on p. 26.)

Every artist, sooner or later, by means of his selective adaptive sense, finds a method in the [26]use of line to suit his own personality—to suit his own individual aim in artistic expression—and in course of time it becomes a characteristic manner, by which his work is instantly known, like a friend's handwriting.

Now what determines this choice, this personal selection, over and above necessities of method and material, it would be difficult to say, unless [27]we had more minute knowledge of the natural history of a human being than we are likely to possess. We can only say that from practice are evolved certain methods or principles, consciously or unconsciously; and it is only these general methods or principles that can be explained and tested for the benefit of those essaying to follow the arduous and difficult path of art.

Relation of Line to Form

At the outset we see that we need a means of definition in drawing, just as a child needs a word to express a thing it wants.*Line*, at the point of the pencil, pen, or brush, places this possibility of definition within our reach; but before we can grasp it we need some knowledge, however rudimentary, of its inseparable companion, *Form.*

I recall two innocent and entertaining methods from the traditions of the nursery, which appeal at once in a curious way to both the oral and graphic senses, and unite story and picture in one. These are illustrated on p. 28. By such devices a child learns to associate line and form, unconsciously and step by step defining form in the use of, or pursuit of, line.[28]

It would be very entertaining and agreeable if we could carry the principle further, and get a passable study from the antique, for instance, by a similar process. In line-drawing we may, however, always tell some story or fact, or character, phase, or idea.

The Graphic Purpose

But supposing we have mounted our steed*Form*, and taken our bridle *Line* in hand, and have started riding at large in the vast domain of nature, with the primary object of finding and hunting down truth at last; we soon perceive that there [29]are so many truths, or rather that truth, even of natural fact, has so many sides, that it is difficult to make up our mind which one to pursue. Thought, however, will soon discover that in this pursuit of truth we strike a road that naturally divides itself, or branches out, into two main paths distinct in aim. These two paths in art have been called by many names; they occasionally cross each other, or overlap, and are sometimes blended, or even confused; but it will be useful for our present purpose to keep them very distinct. I will term them, for convenience:

1. The Graphic Purpose. (Accidental form.)
2. The Ornamental Purpose. (Typical form.)

Our use of line will largely depend upon which of these two it is our object to pursue. Now when we look at anything with intent to draw—say a leafy bough as it grows in the sunshine—we see great complexity of form and surface-lighting. The leaves, perhaps, take all manner of variations of the typical form, and are set at all sorts of angles. In making a rapid sketch with the object of getting the appearance of the bough, we naturally dwell upon these accidents and superficial facts. At the same time, with nothing but line to express them, we are compelled to use a kind of convention, though our aim be purely naturalistic, to get a faithful portrait of the bough.

We must make our line as *descriptive* as possible, defining the main forms boldly, and blocking in broadly the main masses of form and light and shade. We are now aiming at the general look of the thing. We are striving to grasp the facts[30]of *Aspect.* We are concerned with the purely graphic purpose, to make a picture upon paper.

We cannot, however, even under these simple [31]conditions, altogether leave out of account considerations which, strictly speaking, must be termed "decorative." For instance, there is the question of placing the study well upon the paper, a very important point to start with; and then the question of beauty must arise, not only in the selection of our point of view, but in the choice of method, in the treatment of line we adopt; and it does not follow that the most apparently forcible way of getting bold projection by means of black shadows, at the cost of the more delicate characteristics of our subject, is the best. On the contrary, the finest draughtsmanship is always the most subtle and delicate, and one cannot get subtle and delicate draughtsmanship without faithful study and careful constant practice—*knowledge of form*, in short—and I am afraid there is no short cut to it.

The Ornamental Purpose

Now supposing we make our study of leaves, not as an end in itself, and for its simple pictorial values or qualities only, but with an ornamental or decorative purpose in view, intending to make use of its form and character in some more or less systematic design or pattern-work—adapted to special methods and materials—intended to decorate a wall-surface or a textile, for instance; we might certainly start with a general sketch of its appearance as before, but we should find that we should want to understand it in its detail; the law of its growth and construction; we should want to dwell upon its typical character and form, the controlling lines of its masses, rather than on its accidental aspects, because it would really be only with these that we could successfully deal in [32]adapting anything in nature to the conditions and limitations of a design. To do this requires as much art as to make a clever graphic sketch, perhaps more; but it is certainly not so easily[33]understood and appreciated, as a rule. Pattern-work is taken so much for granted, except by those technically interested, whereas a graphic sketch may bring the drama of nature, and of human character and incident, before our eyes. It does not require us to stop and think out the less obvious meaning, or trace the invention or grace of line, to appreciate the rhythmic, silent music which the more formalized and abstract decorative design may contain, *quite apart from the forms it actually represents.*

[34]
[35]

Question and Answer in Line

Here we discover another function of line. For, directly we endeavour to construct a decorative design—that is, a design intended to adorn or to express an object or surface—we find that we must build it upon some sort of a plan, or geometric controlling network or scaffolding, so as to give it unity, rhythm, and coherence—especially so in the case of repeating designs. Even in an isolated panel or picture the necessity of this linear basis will be felt, since one cannot draw a line or define a form without demanding an answer—that is, a corresponding, re-echoing line or mass.

The curve (1. Q) is a proposition or question. It is answered or balanced by the corresponding curve (2. A), and forms the basis for a scroll design.

The five radiating lines (1) are obviously incomplete by themselves, but if we add another [36]four, in reverse order, (2) we get a centred and symmetric motive of an anthemion character.

Wall-Paper Design

Take, however, a wall-paper. The problem is to construct a design pleasant to the eye in line, form, colour, and suggestion; which will be interesting in detail, and yet repeat upon a wall-surface without flaw, and without becoming wearisome. Moreover, one which will lend itself to being cut upon wood, if for block-printing, and which may be reproduced with a due regard to economy of means. The designer may have a square of twenty-one inches in which to make his design.

A useful way to begin with is to rule out a sheet of paper into squares, say on the scale of 1-½ inch to the foot, and upon this jot down your first ideas of linear arrangement and colour motive, and get [37]the general effect, and test the plan of repeats. When you are satisfied with one, enlarge it to full size, correct and amplify it, and improve it in form and detail. Changes will probably be found necessary in drawing it upon the larger scale, sometimes additions, sometimes omissions. Now in sketching out the general plan, one builds, as before said, upon some basis or plan, however simple, since one cannot put a simple spot, sprig, or spray upon [38]paper intending to repeat, without some system of connection to put them into relation.

Controlling Forms

In designing one's sprig, too, the best plan to secure good decorative effect is to see that its general form is inclosed or bounded by an agreeable linear shape, although itself not actually visible. Simple leaf and flower forms are generally the best to use for these controlling boundaries. Sprays designed on this principle may be relied upon for repeating pleasantly and safely when they are placed upon, and connected by, the controlling geometric plan. A good practical test of the truth and completeness of your square repeat is, when the design is done, or even in progress, to cut it into four equal parts (supposing it to be a twenty-one inch square). This will enable you to get the joints true, and also, by altering the position of the squares, to give you a very good idea of the effect of the repeat full size. (See the diagrams on p.41.)

These things must be considered, of course, merely as practical aids to invention: not by any means as substitutes for it. One cannot give any recipe for designing, and no rules, principles, or methods can supply the place of imagination and fancy. "He who would bring back health from the Indies," says an old proverb, "must take it out with him."

At the same time the imagination can be enfeebled by starvation and neglect. It can be depressed by dull and sordid surroundings. It is apt to grow, like other living things, by what it feeds on, and is stronger for exercise and development.

[39]

Memory

Memory, too, is an important and serviceable thing in designing, and this, again, can be cultivated to an almost unlimited extent. I mean that selective kind of memory which, by constant and close observation, extracts and stores up the essential serviceable kind of facts for the designer: facts of form, of structure, of movement of figures, expressive lines, momentary or transitory effects of colour—all those rare and precious visual moments which will not wait, and which happen unexpectedly. They should be captured like rare butterflies and carefully stored in the mind's museum of suggestions, as well as, as far as is [40]possible, pinned down in the hieroglyphics of the note-book.

Evolution in Design

As regards procedure in working out a design, one generally thinks of some leading feature, some central mass or form or curve—of a figure or a flower, say—and one thinks of its capacity in repeat; and, since one form or line should inevitably suggest or necessitate—as by a kind of logic—another, one adds other forms until the design is complete. For it must never be forgotten that design is a growth which has its own stages of evolution in the mind, answering to the evolution of the living forms of nature—first the blade, then the ear, after that the full corn in the ear.

Experience teaches us that the most harmonious arrangements of form and line are those in which the leading lines and forms through all sorts of variations, continually recur. We cannot place a number of sharply contrasting and contradictory forms together in design satisfactorily—at least we cannot do so without recourse to other elements to harmonize and to bring them into relation. For instance, we might get a great deal of ornamental variety by means of a number of heraldic devices upon shields, full in themselves of quaintness and contrasts, but brought into harmony by the boundary lines of the shields and the divisions; or, still further, by throwing them upon a background of leaves and stems, the meandering lines and recurring forms of which would answer as a kind of warp upon which to weave the heraldic spots into a connected and harmonious pattern.

[41]

Variety in Unity

But even in the ornamental treatment of diverse forms, as the mediæval heraldic designers were [42]well aware, they can be brought into decorative harmony by following a similar principle to the one already laid down in regard to the designing of sprigs and sprays: that is to say, that in designing an animal or figure for heraldry or introduction into a pattern, one should arrange it so that it should fall within the boundary of some geometric or foliated form, square, circular, elliptical or otherwise, [43]as might be desirable. To this, however, I hope to return in a future chapter.

Counterbalance

We may here consider another important principle [44]in designing with line and mass, that of *counterbalance.*

Take any defined space as a panel, tile, or border to be filled with design: you place your principal mass, and instantly feel that it must be balanced by a corresponding mass, or some equivalent. Its place will be determined by the principle upon which the design is built. If on a symmetrical arrangement, you find your centre (say of a panel), and you may either throw the chief weight and mass of the design upon the central feature (as a tree), and balance it by smaller forms or wings each side, or *vice versâ*; or, adopting a diagonal plan, you place your principal mass (say it is a tile) near the top left-hand corner (suppose it is a pomegranate), connecting it with a spiral diagonal line (the stem); the place of the counterbalancing mass (the second pomegranate) is obviously near the bottom right-hand corner of the square. You may then feel the necessity for additional smaller forms, and so add to it (the leaves), completing the design. (See preceding page.)

Linear Logic

On the same principle one may design upon various other plans. The exact choice of the distribution of the counterbalancing masses must always be a matter of personal feeling, judgment, and taste, controlled by the perception of certain logical necessities: as it seems to me that designing is a species of linear reasoning,[1] and might almost be worked in its elementary stages on the principle of the syllogism, consisting of two propositions and a conclusion. A spiral curve is a [45]harmonious line, says the designer: repeat it, reversed, and you prolong the harmony; repeat it again, with variations, and you complete the harmony. Or, harmonious effect is produced by recurring form and line. Here is a circular form; here is a meandering line: combine and repeat them, and you get a logical and harmonious border motive.

[1]I recall here a saying of Sir E. Burne-Jones, that "a bad line can only be answered by a good line."

Recurring Line and Form

The everlastingly recurring egg and dart moulding and the volute are instances of the harmonious effect of very simple arrangements of recurring line and form. We also get illustrated in these another linear quality in design—that up-and-down movement which gives a pleasant rhythm to the [46]simplest border, and is of especial consequence in all repeating border and frieze designs. The borders of early, ancient, and classical art might be said to be little besides rhythmical and logical arrangements of line. The same rhythmical principle is found in the designs of the classical frieze in all its varieties, culminating in the rhythmic movement of the great Pan-Athenaic procession in that master-frieze of the Parthenon, which, though full of infinite variety and delicate sculptured detail, is yet controlled by a strictly ornamental motive, and constructed upon the rhythmic recurrence of pure line.

The Principle of Radiation

Another great linear principle in design is what is known as the *radiating* principle, which gives vitality and vigour alike to both arrangements of line and delineations of form. It is emphatically and abundantly illustrated in natural forms, from the scallop shell upon the sea-shore to the sun [47]himself that radiates his light upon it. The palm-leaf in all its graceful varieties demonstrates its beauty, its constructive strength combined with extraordinary lightness, which becomes domesticated in that fragile sceptre of social influence and festivity, the fan, and which again spreads its silken, or gossamer, wing as a suggestive field for the designer. We find the principle springing to life again in the fountain jet, and symbolical of life as it has ever been; by means of the same principle applied to construction the Gothic architects raised their beautiful vaults, and emphasized the structural principle and the beauty of recurring line by moulding the edges of their ribs; while we have but to look at the structure of the human frame to find the same principle there also, in the fibres of the muscles, for instance, the radiation of the ribs, and of the fingers and toes.

In truth, as I have said, if there can be said to be one principle more than another, the perception and expression of which gives to an artist's work in design peculiar vitality, it is this principle of radiating line. One may follow it through all stages and forms of drawing and design, and it is equally important in the design of the figure, in the structure of a flower, in the folds of drapery, and alike in the controlling lines of pictorial composition and decorative plan, whether the lines radiate from seen or from hidden centres, which in all kinds of informal design are perhaps the most important.

Range and Use of Line

We see, therefore, that line possesses a constructive and controlling function, in addition to its power of graphic expression and decorative [48]definition. It is the beginning and the end of art. By means of its help we guide our first tottering steps in the wide world of design; and, as we gain facility of hand and travel further afield, we discover that we have a key to unlock the [49]wonders of art and nature, a method of conjuring up all forms at will: a sensitive language capable of recording and revealing impressions and beauties of form and structure hidden from the careless eye: a delicate instrument which may catch and [50]perpetuate in imperishable notation unheard harmonies: a staff to lean upon through the journey of life: a candid friend who never deceives us: perchance a divining rod, which may ultimately reveal to us that Beauty and Truth are one—as they certainly are, or ought to be, in the world of art.

[51]

CHAPTER III

Of the Choice and Use of Line—Degree and Emphasis—Influence of the Photograph—The Value of Emphasis—The Technical Influence—The Artistic Purpose—Influence of Material and Tools—Brush-work—Charcoal—Pencil—Pen.

RECOGNIZING the great range and capacity of line as a means of expression, and also the range of choice it presents to the designer and draughtsman, the actual exercise of this choice of line, with a view to the most expressive and effective use in practice, becomes, of course, of the first consequence.

In this matter of choice we are helped by natural bias, by personal character and preferences, for which it would, as I have said, be difficult fully to account; but beyond this a kind of evolution goes on, arising out of actual practice, which controls and is controlled by it. Draw simply a succession of strokes with any point upon paper, and we find that we are gradually led to repeat a particular kind of stroke, a particular degree of line, partly perhaps because it seems to be produced with more ease, and partly because it appears to have the pleasantest effect.

Choice of Line

By a kind of "natural selection," therefore, influenced no doubt by many small secondary causes, such as the relation of the particular angle of the [52]hand and pencil-point to the surface—the nature of the point itself and the nature of the surface—we finally arrive at a choice of line. This choice, [53]again, will be liable to constant variation, owing to the nature of the object we are about to draw, or the kind of design we want to make.

Use of Line

The kind of line which seems appropriate to representing the delicate edges of a piece of low-relief sculpture, for instance, would require greater force and firmness if we wanted to draw an antique cast in the round, and in strong light and shade. The character of our line should be sympathetic with the character of our subject as far as possible, and sensitive to its differences of character and surface, since it is in this sensitiveness that the expressive power and peculiar virtue of line-drawing consists.

A feather, a lily, a scallop shell, all show as an essential principle of their form and construction the radiating line; but what a different quality of line would be necessary to express the differences of each: for the soft, yet firm, smooth flowing curves of the feather fibres no line would be too delicate; and the lily would demand no less delicacy, and even greater precision and firmness of curve, while a slight waviness, or quiver, in the lines might express the silken or waxy surface of the petals; while a crustier, more rugged, though equally firm line would be wanted to follow the rigid furrows and serrated surface of the shell. The leaves of trees and plants of all kinds, which perhaps afford the best sort of practice in line-drawing at first, present in their varieties of structure, character, and surfaces continual opportunities for the exercise of artistic judgment in the choice and use of line.

The forms and surfaces of fruits, again, are [54]excellent tests of line draughtsmanship, and their study is a good preparation for the more subtle and delicate contours of the human form—the greatest test of all. Here we see firmness of fundamental structure (in the bones) and surface curve (of sinew and muscle), with a mobile and constantly changing surface (of flesh and sensitive skin). To render such characteristics without tending to overdo either the firmness or the mobility, and so to become too rigid on the one hand, or too loose and indefinite on the other, requires extraordinary skill, knowledge, and practice in the use of line. I do not suppose the greatest master ever satisfied himself yet in this direction.

Degree and Emphasis

When we have settled upon our quality of line and its *degree*—thick or thin, bold or fine—we shall be met with the question of *emphasis*, for upon this the ultimate effect and expression of our[55]drawing or design must largely depend. In the selection of any subject we should naturally be influenced by the attractiveness of particular parts, characters, or qualities it might possess, and we should direct our efforts towards bringing these out, as the things which impress us most. That is the difference between the mind and hand working together harmoniously and the sensitized plate in the photographic camera, which, uncontrolled in any way by human choice (and even under that control as it always is to some extent), mechanically registers the action of the light rays which define the impress of natural forms and scenes through the lens focussed upon the plate. So that, as we often see in a photograph, some unimportant or insignificant detail is reproduced with as much distinctness (or more) as are the leading figures or whatever form the interesting features or the motive of the subject. The picture suffers from want of emphasis, or from emphasis in the wrong place. It is, of course, here that the art of the photographer comes in; and, although he can by careful selection, arrangement, and the regulation of exposure, largely counteract the mechanical tendency, a photograph by its very nature can never take the place of a work of art—the first-hand expression, more or less abstract, of a human mind, or the creative inner vision recorded by a human hand.

Influence of the Photograph

Photography does wonders, and for certain qualities of light and shade, and form and effect without colour, no painting or drawing can approach it; but it has the value and interest of science rather than of art. It is invaluable to the [56]student of natural fact, surface effect, and momentary action, and is often in its very failures most interesting and suggestive to artists—who indeed have not been slow to avail themselves of the help of photography in all sorts of ways. Indeed the wonder is, considering its services to art in all directions, how the world could ever have done without it.

But a photograph cannot do everything. It cannot make original designs, and it cannot draw in line. You can design in the solid, and make your groups in the studio or the open air; you can select your point of view, and the photograph will reproduce. You can make your drawing in line, and it will copy it; and we know its sphere of usefulness in this direction is enormous, since it can bring before our eyes the whole range of ancient art.

In short, photography is an excellent servant and friend, but a dangerous master. It may easily beguile us by its seductive reproductions of surface relief and lighting to think more of these qualities than any other, and to endeavour to put them in the wrong places—in places where we want colour planes rather than shadow planes, flatness and repose rather than relief, for instance, as mostly in surface decoration.

But one way of learning the value of emphasis is to draw from a photograph, and it will soon be discovered what a difference in expression is produced by dwelling a little more here, or a little less there.

The Value of Emphasis

In designing, the use of emphasis is very important; and it may be said that drawing or designing [57]without emphasis is like reading without stops, while awkward emphasis is like putting your stops in the wrong place.

By a difference in emphasis the same design may be given quite a different effect and expression.

Suppose, for instance, we were designing a vertical pattern of stem, leaves, and fruit in one colour. By throwing the emphasis upon the leaves, as in No. 1, we should gain one kind of effect or decorative expression. By throwing the emphasis upon the fruit, and leaving the leaves in outline, we should get quite a different effect out of the same elements, as in No. 2.

While by leaving stem, leaves, and fruit all in outline, and throwing the emphasis upon the ground, we should get, again, a totally distinct kind of effect and expression.

Similar differences of effect and expression, [58]owing to differences of emphasis, might be studied in the drawing and treatment of a head (as in A, B, and C). The possibilities of such variations of emphasis in drawing are practically unlimited and co-extensive with the variations of expression we see in nature herself. The pictorial artist is free to translate or represent them in his work, controlled solely by the conditions and purpose of his work.

It is these conditions and purposes which really control both choice and treatment, and determine the emphasis, and therefore the expression of the work.

No kind of art can be said to be unconditioned, and the simplest and freest of all, *the art of the point and the surface*, which covers all the graphic art and flat designing, is still subject to certain technical influences, and it may be said that it is very much in so far as these technical influences or conditions are acknowledged and utilized that the work gains in artistic character.

[SN The Technical Influence]

The draughtsman in line who draws for surface printing, for the book or newspaper, should be able to stand the test of the peculiar conditions; and, so [59]far from attempting to escape them, and seeking something more than they will bear, should welcome them as incentives to a distinct artistic treatment with a value and character of its own, which indeed all the best work has. It is, for instance, important in all design associated with type for surface printing, that there should be a certain harmonious relation between lettering or type and printer's ornament or picture.

[60]

[61]

[62]A firm and open quality of line, with bright black and white effects, not only has the most attractive decorative effect with type, but lends itself to the processes of reproduction for surface printing best, whether woodcut or one of the numerous forms of so-called automatic photo-engraving, as well as to the conditions of the printing press.

In all design-work which has to be subjected to processes of engraving and printing, clearness and definiteness of line is very necessary. Designs for textile printing of all kinds, for wall-papers, especially, require good firm drawing and definite colour planes. This does not, however, mean hardness of effect. A design should be clear and intelligible without being hard.

For weaving, again, definiteness in pattern designing is very necessary, since the design must be capable of being rendered upon the severe conditions of the point paper, by which it is only possible to produce curves by small successive angles (which sounds like a contradiction in terms). The size of these angles or points, of course, varies very much in the different kinds of textile with which pattern is incorporated, from the fine silk fabric, in which they are almost inappreciable, to carpets of all kinds, where they are emphatic; so that a certain squareness of mass becomes a desirable and characteristic feature in designs for these purposes, and, indeed, I think it should be more or less acknowledged in all textile design, in order to preserve its distinctive beauty and character.

The Artistic Purpose

Beauty and character.—In these lies the gist of all design. While the technical conditions, if fully understood, fairly met, and frankly acknowledged, [63]are sure to give *character* to a design, for whatever purpose, *beauty* is not so easy to command. It is so delicate a quality, so complex in its elements, a question often of such nice balance and judgment—depending perhaps upon a hair's-breadth difference in the poise of a mass here, or the sweep of a curve there—that we cannot weave technical nets fine enough to catch so sensitive a butterfly. She is indeed a Psyche in art, both seeking and sought, to be finally won only by devotion and love.

This search for beauty—this Psyche of art—is the purely inspiring artistic purpose, as distinct from the technical and useful one, which should, perfectly reconciled and united with it, determine the form of our work.

In drawing or design we may seek particular qualities in line and form either of representation or of ornament. We may desire to dwell upon particular beauties either of object or subject. Say, in drawing from a cast or from natural form of any kind, we desire to dwell upon beauty of line or quality of surface. Well, since it is most difficult, if not impossible, to get everything at once, and nothing without some kind of sacrifice, we shall find that to give prominence to—to bring out—the particular quality in our subject (say beauty of line), it becomes necessary to subordinate other qualities to this. A drawing in pure outline of a figure may be a perfect thing in itself. The moment we begin to superadd shading, or lines expressive of relief of any kind, we introduce another element; we are aiming at another kind of truth or beauty; and unless we have also a distinctly ideal aim in this, we shall mar the simplicity of the outline without gaining [64]any compensating advantage, or really adding to the truth or beauty of the drawing.

In designing, too, unless we can so contrive the essential characteristics of our pattern that they shall be adaptable to the method and material of its production, and make its reproduction quite practicable, it is sure to reappear more or less marred and incomplete. The thing is to discover what kind of character and beauty the method will allow of—whether beauty or quality of line, or surface, or colour, or material; and if to be reproduced in a particular method or material, the design should be thought out in the method or material for which it is destined, rather than as a drawing on paper, and worked out accordingly, using every opportunity to secure the particular kind of beauty naturally belonging to such work in its completed form.

Thus we should naturally think of *planes of surface* in modelled work, and the delicate play of light and shade, getting our equivalent for colour in the design and contrast of varied surfaces. In stained glass we should think of a pattern in lead lines inclosing one of translucent colour, each being interdependent and united to form a harmonious whole. In textile design we should be influenced by the thought of the difference of use, plan, and purpose of the finished material; as the difference between a rich vertical pattern in silk, velvet, or tapestry, to be broken by folds as in curtains or hangings, and a rich carpet pattern, to be spread upon the unbroken level surface of a floor. The idea of the wall and floor should here influence us as well as the actual technical necessities of the loom. It would be part of the artistic purpose [65]affecting the imagination and artistic motive, and working with the strictly technical conditions.

The mind must project itself, and see with the inner eye the effect of the design as it would appear in actual use, as far as possible. Invention, knowledge, and experience will do the rest.

Brush-Work

Keeping, however, to strictly pictorial or graphic conditions—to the art of the point and the surface—with which, as designers and draughtsmen, we are more immediately concerned, we cannot forget certain technical considerations strictly belonging to the varieties of point and of surface, and their relations one to another. The flexible point of the brush, for instance, dipped in ink, or colour, has its own peculiar capacity, its own range of treatment, one might say, its own forms.

The management admits of immense variation of use and touch, and its range of depicting and ornamental power are very great: from the simpler leaf forms, which seem to be almost a reflection or shadow of the moist pointed brush itself, to the elaborate graphic drawing in line or light and shade.

In forming the leaf shape one begins with a light pressure, if at the point, and proceeds to increase it for the middle and broader end. On the same principle of regulation of pressure any brush forms may be built up. It is essential for freedom in working with the brush not to starve or stint it in moisture or colour. For ornamental forms a full brush should be used: otherwise they are apt to look dragged and meagre. For a rich and flowing line also a full brush, however fine, is necessary. It is quite possible, however, to use it with a different [66]aim, and to produce a sort of crumbling line when half dry, and also in colour-work for what is called dragging, by which tone, texture, or quality may [67]be given to parts of a drawing. One should never lose sight, in using the brush as a drawing tool, of its distinctive quality and character, and impart it to all work done by its means.

[68]The direct touch with the full brush—to cultivate this is of enormous advantage to all artists, whatever particular line of art they may follow, since it may be said to be of no less value in design than it is in painting pure and simple. We can all feel the charm of the broad brush washes and emphatic brush touches of a master of water-colour landscape such as De Wint. This is mastery of brush and colour in one direction—tone and effect. A Japanese drawing of a bird or a fish may show it equally in another—character and form. A bit of Oriental porcelain or Persian tile may show the same dexterous charm and full-brush feeling exercised in a strictly decorative direction.

[69]

The empire of the brush, if we think of it in all its various forms and directions, is very large; and it commands, in skilled hands, both *line* and *form*, in all their varieties, and leaves its impress in all the departments of art, from the humble but dexterous craftsman who puts the line of gold or colour round the edges of our cups and saucers, to the highly skilled and specialized painter of easel pictures—say the academician who writes cheques with his paint-brush!

Charcoal and Pencil

Then we have the ordinary varieties of the firm point: charcoal, pencil, pen. Charcoal, being halfway between hard and soft—a sort of halfway house or bridge for one passing from the flexible brush to the firm and hard points of pencil and pen—is first favourite with painters when they take to drawing. Its softness and removability adapts it as a tool for preliminary and preparatory sketching in for all purposes, and both for designer and painter; but it lends itself to both line and [70]tone drawing, or to a mixture of both. It is therefore a very good material for rapid studies (say from the life) and the seizing of any effect of light and shade rapidly, since the masses can be laid in readily, and greater richness and depth can be obtained in shorter time, perhaps, than by any other kind of pencil.

Charcoal is also very serviceable for large cartoon-work, since it is capable of both delicacy and force, and bears working up to any extent. A slight rubbing of the finger gives half tones when wanted, and is often serviceable in giving greater solidity and finish to the work.

Then there is the lead pencil—the point-of-all-work, as it might be called—more generally serviceable than any other, whether for rapid sketches and jottings in the note-book, or careful and detailed drawings, or sketching in for the smaller kinds of design-work. It is also, of course, used for drawings which are afterwards "inked in." I do not think, however, that pen-work done in this way is so free or characteristic as when done direct, or at any rate quite freely, upon a mere scaffolding of preliminary lines, used only to make the plans for the chief masses and forms.

Pencil drawing is capable of being carried to a greater pitch of delicacy and finish, and has a silvery quality all its own. It has not the force or range of charcoal, but in its own technical range it possesses many advantages. Its gray and soft line, however charming in itself, does not fit it for work where sharpness and precision of line and touch are required, as may be said to [71]be the case with all work intended to be reproduced by some process of handicraft or manufacture, except some sorts of photo-engraving or lithography. We must therefore look to another implement to enable us to obtain these qualities, namely, the brush, the use and qualities of which I have already touched upon.

The Pen

There remains yet another point of the firm and decisive order, the pen, which enables us to get firmness and sharpness of line and precise definition, as well as considerable range of treatment and freedom of touch.

The pen seems to bear much the same relation to the brush as the lead pencil does to charcoal—not capable of such full and rich effects or such flowing freedom of line, but yet possessing its own beauty and characteristic kinds of expression. Its true province is in comparatively small scale work, and its natural association is with its sister-pen of literature in the domain of book-design and decoration, and black and white drawing for the press. Its varieties are endless, and the ingenuity of manufacturers continually places before us fresh choice of pen-points to work with; but though one occasionally meets with a good steel pen, I have found it too often fails one just when it is sufficiently worn to the right degree of flexibility. One returns to the quill, which can be cut to suit the particular requirements of one's work. For large bold drawing the reed-pen has advantages, and a pleasant rich quality of line.

But with whatever point we may work, the great object is to be perfectly at ease with it in drawing—to thoroughly master its use and capacities, [72]so that in our search for that other command, of line and form, we may feel that we have in our hands a tool upon which we can rely, a trusty spear to bear down the many difficulties and discouragements that beset, like threatening dragons, the path of the art-student.

[73]

CHAPTER IV

Of the Choice of Form—Elementary Forms—Space-filling—Grouping—Analogies of Form—Typical Forms of Ornament—Ornamental Units—Equivalents in Form—Quantities in Design—Contrast—Value of Variations of Similar or Allied Forms—Use of the Human Figure and Animal Forms in Ornamental Design.

WE were considering the choice and use of Line in the last chapter: its expressive characters and various methods. We now come to the no less important question to the designer and draughtsman—*The Choice of Form.*

If Line may be said to be the bone and sinew of design, Form is the substance and the flesh, and both are obviously essential to its free life and development.

Elementary Forms

The *cube* and the *sphere* give us the fundamental elements, or primal types from which are derived the multifarious, ever varying, and complex forms, the products of the forces and conditions of nature, or the necessitous inventiveness of art, just as we may take the square and the circle to be the parents of linear and geometric design.

The cube and the sphere, the ellipse, the cone, and the pyramid, with other comparatively simple forms of solid geometry, present themselves to [74]the student as elementary tests of draughtsmanship—of the power, that is, of representing solid bodies upon a plane surface. Such forms being more simple and regular than any natural forms, they are supposed to reduce the problem of drawing to its simplest conditions. They certainly afford very close tests of correctness of eye, making any fault in perspective or projection at once apparent.

[76]To avoid, however, falling into mechanical ways, and to maintain the interest and give vitality to such studies, the relation of such forms to forms in nature and art should be borne in mind, and no opportunity missed of comparing them, or of seeking out their counterparts, corresponding principles, and variations, as well as their practical bearing, both functional and constructive; as in the case of the typical forms of flowers, buds, and seed-vessels, for instance, where the cone and the funnel, and the spherical, cylindrical, and tubular principles are constantly met with, as essential parts of the characters and organic necessities of the plant: the cone and the funnel mostly in buds and flower-petals for protection and inclosure of the pollen and seed germs, the tube for conducting the juices; the spherical form to resist moisture externally, or to hold it internally, or to avoid friction, and facilitate close storage, as in the case of seeds in pods. The seed-vessel of the poppy, for instance, has a curious little pent-house roof to shield the interstices (like windows in a tower) till the seed is ripe and the time comes for it to be shaken out of the shell or pod. A further practical reason for the prevalence of spherical form in seeds is that they may, when the outer covering or husk perishes, more readily roll out and fall into the interstices of the ground; or when, as in the case of various fruits, such as the apple and orange, the envelope

itself is spherical and intended to carry their flat or pointed seeds to the ground, where it falls and rolls when ripe.

[75]

The cube and the various multiple forms may [77]be found in crystals and basaltic rocks, as well as in organic nature, as, for instance, in the honeycomb of bees, where choice of form is a constructive necessity: the cube is in every sense of the word the corner-stone in architecture, and without squaring and plumbing no building could be constructed, while the cylindrical and conical principles of form are illustrated in towers and roofs, spires and pinnacles. In architectural ornament and carved decoration the cube and sphere again form the basis, both forming ornaments themselves by mere recurrence and repetition, and also forming constructional bases of ornament.

Dog-Tooth Ornament

A very simple but effective form of carved [78]ornament characteristic of early Gothic work is what is known as the dog-tooth. This is formed simply by cutting a cube of stone into a pyramid, depressing the sides, and cutting them into geometric leaves, leaving the sharp angles of the pyramid from the base to the apex standing out in bold relief. In ground-plan this is simply composed geometrically of a rectangle divided diagonally into four equal parts, and by striking four semicircles from the centres of the four sides of the rectangle. Here we get a form of ornament [79]in the flat which appears to have been very widely used, and reappears in the early art of nearly all races so far as I am aware. We find it, for instance, in Assyrian carving and in early Greek decoration, in China and Japan, and in European mediæval work of all kinds. Its charm perhaps lies in its simplicity of construction yet rich ornamental effect, either as carved work or as a flat painted diaper. It might also be used as the geometric basis of an elaborate repeating wall-pattern over a large surface.

Filling of Spaces

When it comes to the choice of form, when we are face to face with a particular problem in design, ornament, or decoration (say, as most frequently happens, it is to fill a panel of a given shape and size), we are bound to consider form in relation to that particular panel, to the subject we propose to treat, and the method by which the design is to be produced, or the object and position for which it is intended. This generally narrows the range of possible choice. Firstly, there is the shape of the panel itself. A well-known exercise for the Teacher's Certificate under the Department of Science and Art is to give a drawing of a plant adapted to design in a square and a circle. Now in the abstract one would be inclined to select for a circular fitting different forms from those one might select for a square filling, since I always consider that the shape of the space must influence the character of the filling in line and form. Still, if the problem is to fill a square and a circle by the same forms, or an adaptation of them, we must rely more and more upon difference of *treatment* of these forms, and not try to [80]squeeze round forms into rectangular space, or rectangular forms into circular space. In a rose, for instance, it would be possible to dwell on its angular side for the square, and on its curvilinear side for the circle. Anyway, we should seek in the first place a good and appropriate motive.

Supposing the design is for wood inlay, we should have to select forms that would not cause unnecessary difficulty in cutting, since every form in the design would have to be cut out in thin wood and inserted in the corresponding hollow cut in the panel or plank to receive it. Complex or complicated forms would therefore be ruled out, as being [81]not only difficult or impossible to reproduce in the material, but ineffective.

Inlay Design

A true feeling for the particular effect and decorative charm of inlaid work should lead us to limit ourselves to comparatively few and simple forms, treating those forms in an emphatic but abstract way, and making use of recurring line and form as far as possible. We might make an effective panel, say, for a casket, or a clock-case, or a floor, by strictly limiting ourselves to very few and simple forms—say, for instance, a stem, a leaf, a berry, or disc, and a bird form, or fruit and leaf forms. It would be possible to build up a design with such elements both pleasant in effect and well adapted to the [82]work. An excellent plan would be to cut out all one's forms with knife or scissors in stiff paper, as a test of the practicability of an inlay design. This is actually done with the working drawing by the inlay cutter.

[83]I once designed an inlaid floor for the centre of a picture gallery. The scale was rather large, and the work was bold. One kept to large, bold, and simple forms—water-lilies and broad leaves, swans, scallop shells, and zigzag borders. Forms which can be readily produced by the brush would generally answer well for inlay, since they would have simple and sweeping boundaries and flat silhouette. And for inlay one is practically designing in black, white, or tinted silhouette. This makes it very good practice for all designers, both for the invention it tends to call out, owing to the limited resources and restriction as to forms, and also as giving facility and readiness in blocking in the masses of pattern.

The water-colour painter, too, would find that blocking in in flat local colour all his forms and the colours of his background was an excellent method of preparatory work, and afforded good practice in direct painting, since he could add his secondary shades and tints in the same manner until the work was brought to completion, while preserving that fresh effect of the undisturbed washes which is the great charm of water-colour.

Grouping of Allied Forms

In seeking forms to group together harmoniously—which is the whole object of composition—we shall find that much the same kind of principle holds good whether we are arranging a still-life group or designing a wall-paper or textile. It is only a difference of degree and scale. In the one case we are designing in the solid with the actual objects, before drawing or painting them as a harmonious pictorial composition; in the other we are arranging forms upon the flat with a view to harmonious composition with a strictly decorative purpose [84]in view. In the first we are dealing with concrete form in the round; in the second, generally speaking, with abstract form in the flat.

But in either case we want harmony. We cannot, therefore, throw together a number of forms unrelated to each in line, contour, or meaning. We seek in composing or designing not contradictions, but correspondences of form, with just an element of contrast to give flavour and point. In grouping pottery, for instance, we should not place big and little or squat and slender forms close together without connecting links of some kind. We want a series of good lines that help one another and lead up to one another in a kind of friendly co-operation. Broad smooth forms and rounded surfaces, again, require relief and a certain amount of [85]contrast. We feel the need of crisp leaves or flowers, perhaps, with our pottery form. We may safely go far, however, on the principle of grouping similar or allied forms, giving our composition as a whole either a curvilinear or angular character in its general lines, masses, and forms, on the principle of like to like. This will entirely depend upon our choice of grouping of form; but the more by our selection we make our composition tend distinctly in the one direction or the other, the more character it will be likely to possess.

Grouping

In selecting forms for still-life grouping and [86]painting, I think increased interest might be gained by arranging significant objects, accessories bearing upon particular pursuits, for instance, in natural relationship and surrounding. Groups suggesting certain handicrafts, for instance, such as the clear glass globe of the wood-engraver, the sand-bag, [87]the block upon it, the tools, gravers lying around, the eye-glass, an old book of woodcuts, and so forth. Other groups suggestive of various arts and industries could be arranged—such motives as metal-work, pottery, literature, painting, music, embroidery, spring, summer, autumn, and winter, might all be suggestively illustrated by well-selected groups of still life. Even different historic periods might be emblematically suggested—I should like to see more done in this way.

To return to design in the flat. If we start with a motive of circular masses, we cannot suddenly associate them with sharp angles—I mean in our leading forms. Of course we can make a network or trellis or diaper of the angles, to form a mat,[89]ground, or a framework on which to place our broad masses, as we may see effectively done by the Chinese and Japanese.

Corresponding Forms

[88]

If the principal group of forms in our pattern, say, are fruit forms—apples, pomegranates, or oranges—we must re-echo or carry out the curves in a lesser degree in the connecting stems and leaves. Change the form of the fruit, say, to lemons, and a further variation of connecting or subsidiary curve in stems and leaves will naturally suggest itself, and at the same time in following such principles we shall be expressing in an abstract way more of the character of the tree or plant itself. In looking at the leaf of a tree one may often see a suggestion of the general character and contour of the tree itself, and we know the line:

"Just as the twig is bent the tree's inclined."

In dealing with angular motives the same principle would be followed, but corresponding to the difference of motive. Let the form of your detail be reflected in the character of your mass.

I have spoken of the necessity in designing of seeking correspondences in form, and although, could we place every form in proper sequence and supply all the intermediary links to unite them harmoniously, forms of extreme diversity might thus be associated, given great extension of space (as in wall decoration, for instance), even then we should want these forms to correspond and recur. Yet, as a rule, having to deal in design with what are really parts rather than wholes, we can only endeavour by making the design of these parts simple and harmonious in line and form, and true to [92]their special conditions, to render their association decoratively possible.

[90]

[91]

Certain forms seem to lend themselves to design in ornament better than others, because they give the designer certain lines and masses which can be harmoniously repeated or combined with other allied forms or lines. Design from this point of view becomes a search for analogies of form.

Analogies of Form

I mentioned certain simple geometric forms common to nature and art. Early ornament consists in the repetition of such forms. The next step was to connect them by lines: and so form and line, through endless vicissitudes and complexities, became united, to live happily in the world of decorative motive ever after. But long after the primitive unadorned geometric forms themselves have ceased to be the chief forms in ornament, their controlling influence is asserted over the boundaries of the more complicated masses introduced.

Typical Forms of Ornament

The simple rectangle is disguised under the fret, the circle and spiral assert their sway over the boundaries of the palmette, or circle and semicircle unite to form the oval so frequently used both as a unit in Greek ornament and as a controlling boundary. These are typical border forms: for extension and repetition in fields of pattern we find the same geometric plans at work in combination and subdivision, forming at first the ornament itself, and afterwards furnishing the plan and controlling boundaries only. Even in later stages in the evolution of surface decoration, in what are called naturalistic floral patterns, amid apparent carelessness and freedom, by the exigencies of repetition the ghost of buried geometric connection reappears, [94]and compels the most naturalistic roses on a wall-paper to acknowledge themselves artificial after all, as they nod to their counterparts from the masked angles of the inevitable diaper repeat.

[93]

We find in the historical forms of decorative art constantly recurring types of form and line, such as the lotus of the Egyptians, the anthemia of the Greeks, the pineapple-like flower and palmette of the Persians, the peony of the Chinese. These forms, at first valued solely for their symbolical and heraldic significance, and continually demanded, became to the designer important elements or *units* in ornament. They gave him fine sweeping curves, radiating lines, and bold masses, without which a designer cannot live, any more than a poet without words. They were capable, too, of infinite variation in treatment, a variation which has been continued ever since, as by importation to different countries (the movement going on from east to west) the same forms were treated by designers of different races, and became mixed with other native elements, or consciously imitated as they are now by Manchester designers and manufacturers, to be sold again in textile form to their original owners, as it were, in the far East. Truly, a strange turn of the wheel.

Ornamental Units

The range of choice in ornamental units is, indeed, embarrassingly large for the modern designer, and a careful and tasteful selection becomes of more and more importance. It is not the number of forms you can combine, or because they are of Persian or Chinese origin, that your work will be artistic, but the judicious and inventive use made of the elements of your design. Ready-made units, [95]such as the Oriental forms I have mentioned, are no doubt easier to combine, to make an effect with, because a certain amount of selection has already been done. In fact, with such forms as the Persian or Indian palmette, we are dealing with the results of centuries of ornamental evolution, and with emblems immemorially treasured by ancient races. It behoves us, if we are called upon to recombine them, to treat them with sympathy, refinement, and respect, and to let them deteriorate as little as possible, for the spirit of an important ornamental form is like a gathered flower—it soon withers and becomes limp.

Equivalents in Form

It is the *spirit*, after all, that is the important thing to preserve, in decorative design, however widely we may depart from the*letter* sometimes. This is a difficult quality to define, but I should say it chiefly consists in a nice attention to the character of form, the elastic spring of curves, an understanding of the construction and proportions, and grasp of the effect. In designing we constantly feel the need of repeating certain masses with variations or balancing them by equivalents, or the necessity of leading up to certain main forms by subsidiary forms, and to carry out their lines in other parts of the composition. In designing figures or emblems, for instance, within inclosed spaces, such as shields or cartouche shapes, forming leading elements in a design, it requires much invention and ornamental feeling so to arrange them that, while different in subject or meaning, and differently spaced, they shall yet properly counterbalance each other, and, though varied in detail, shall yet be equivalent in quantity. The same sort of feeling would [96]govern the case of designing two masses of fruit and foliage, say, forming two halves of an oblong panel, which, though starting on the symmetric plan from the centre, are not intended to be alike in detail; or in a frieze composed of a series of formalized trees, where it was desired to have each different, say, to express the progression of the seasons, it would be the sense of the necessity of [98]equivalents which would govern the decorative effect.

[97]

Quantities in Design

Such considerations naturally lead us to the question of the use of *quantities* in design—the ornamental proportions of ornament, or the contrasting distribution of form and line. For the mere repetition of ornamental forms over surfaces and objects without reference to proportion or structure is not decoration. The perception of appropriate quantities in design is really the decorative gauge or measure of effect.

In designing a bordered panel—or say a carpet—we [99]might decide to throw the weight of pattern, colour, or emphasis upon either the field or border. Supposing the field had a dark ground upon which the arabesque or floral design was relieved, in the border it would be most effective to transpose this arrangement, making the ground light, and bringing out the border design dark upon it. Or, if the motive were reversed, giving a light ground to the [100]centre, with the pattern dark, the border might be brought out on a dark field. Or, again, for a less emphatic treatment the quantities of the pattern itself might be almost infinitely varied, massive forms and close fillings contrasting with open borders and united with intermediary bands.

These intermediary bands or subsidiary borders are very important in Eastern rugs and carpets, and their quantities very carefully considered. A Persian designer, for instance, would never leave a blank unbroken strip of colour to surround his field; his object is not to isolate the quantities of his pattern, but to distinguish and unite them: so he makes use of the subsidiary borders as additional quantities. [101]A usual arrangement which always looks well is to have the border proper inclosed in two bands of about the same width and quantity in pattern—or they might be a repeat of each other—and to inclose the field or centre within another narrow subsidiary border. But the variations to be observed in any chance selection of Persian rugs or carpets are constant, and the amount of subtle variety and invention in these subsidiary borders is endless.

Very excellent examples of the treatment and distribution of quantities may also be studied in the older Indian printed cottons, such as maybe seen at South Kensington.

Contrast

The consideration of quantities in form and design involves the question of *contrast*, which, indeed, can hardly be separated from it. There is the contrast of form and line, and the contrast of colour and plane. It is with the first kind we are dealing now.

Take the simplest linear border, such as the type common in Greek work. We should easily weary of the continual repetition of such a form alone and unassisted, but add a vertical with an alternative dark filling, and we get a certain richness and solidity which is a relief at once. Add another quantity, and we get the rich effect of the egg and tongue or egg and dart moulding.

A still simpler instance of the use of contrast, however, is the chequer, or the principle of equal alternation of dark and light masses; but this touches colour contrast rather than form.

[102]

The love of contrast makes the Chinese porcelain-painter break the blue borders of his plates [103]with small cartouche-like forms inclosing the light ground, varied with a spray or device of some light kind; or the diagonal, closely-filled field of his woven silk by broad discs or cartouches of another plane of ornament. But the love of sharp or very violent contrasts, more especially of form, may easily lead one astray and be destructive of ornamental effect. Like all decorative considerations, the artistic use of contrast depends much upon the particular case and the conditions of the work, and one cannot lay down any unvarying rules. There are agreeable and disagreeable contrasts, and their choice and use must depend upon the individual artist.

Variation of Allied Forms

The most beautiful kinds of design rather seem to depend upon the harmonious variation in association of similar or allied forms than on sharp contrasts.

In compositions of figures the association of the delicate curves and angles of the human form, and the lines of drapery, with the emphatic verticals and horizontals, the semicircles and rectangles of architectural form, for instance, are always delightful in competent hands; as also compositions of figure and landscape, with its possibilities of undulating line corrected by the severe horizon, or sea-line, and contrasted with the vertical lines of trees, stems, and the rich forms of foliage masses.

For the same reasons both of correspondence and contrast, masses of type or lettering of good form are admirable as foils to figure designs, in which commemorative monuments of all kinds and book designs afford abundant opportunities to the designer.

[106]Use Of Human Figure and Animal Forms

In surface or textile decoration of all kinds nothing gives so much relief and vitality as the judicious use of animal forms and the human figure, although they are not much favoured at present. The forms of birds and animals, if designed in relation to the rest of the pattern, will give a pleasant variety of form and line, and in their forms and lines we find just those elements both of correspondence and contrast, in their relation to geometric or to floral design, which are so valuable.

[104]

In order to combine such forms successfully, however, great care in designing is necessary; and a good sound principle to follow as a general guide is to make the boundaries of the bird or animal touch the limits of an imaginary inclosing form of some simple geometric or floral or leaf shape (see p. 104). This would at once control the form and render it available in a pattern as a decorative mass or unit. The particular shape of the controlling form must, of course, depend upon the general character of the design, whether free and flowing or square and restricted, the nature of the repeat, the ultimate position of the work, and so on. A study of Gothic heraldry and the early Sicilian silk patterns would be very instructive in this connection, since it is rather the heraldic ideal than that of the natural history book which is decoratively appropriate. At the same time it is quite possible to combine ornamental treatment with a great deal of natural truth in structure and character.

[105]

Much the same principles apply to the treatment of the human figure as an element in ornament; they should be designed, whether singly or in groups, under the control of imaginary boundaries, [107]and care must be taken that in line and mass they re-echo (or are re-echoed by) other lines which connect them with the rest of the design, if they occur as incidents in repeating wall-paper or hanging design, for instance. It is, however, quite possible to imagine a decorative effect produced by the use of figures alone (see p. 105), with something very subsidiary in the way of connecting links of linear or floral pattern, much as figures were used by the ancient Greek vase-painters, beautifully distributed as ornament over the concave or convex surfaces of the vases and vessels of the potter, the forms of which, as all good decoration should do, they helped to express as well as to adorn.

[108]

CHAPTER V

Of the Influence of Controlling Lines, Boundaries, Spaces, and Plans in Designing—Origin of Geometric Decorative Spaces and Panels in Architecture—Value of Recurring Line—Tradition—Extension—Adaptability—Geometric Structural Plans—Frieze and Field—Ceiling Decoration—Co-operative Relation.

THE function of line considered from the point of view of its controlling influence as a boundary, or inclosure, of design, upon which I touched in the last chapter, is a very important one, and deserves most attentive study.

The usual problem a designer in the flat has to solve is to fill harmoniously a given space or panel defined by a line—some simple geometric form—such as a square or a circle, a parallelogram, a diamond, a lunette.

Influence of Controlling Lines, etc.

Now it is possible to regard such spaces or panels as more or less unrelated, and simply as the boundaries of an individual composition or picture of some kind. Yet even so considered a certain sense of geometric control would come in in the selection of our lines and masses, both in regard to each other and in regard to the shape of the inclosing boundary. We seem to feel the need of some answering line or re-echo in the character of the composition to the shape of its boundary, to give it its [110]distinctive reason for existence in that particular form—just as we should expect a shell-fish to conform to the shape of its shell. Such a re-echo or acknowledgment might be ever so slight, or might be quite emphatic and dominate as the leading motive, but for perfectly harmonious effect it must be there.

[109]

A strictly simple and logical linear filling of such spaces might be expressed in the most primitive way, as in the illustration on p. 109.

By these means certain primitive types of ornament are evolved, such as the Greek volute and the Greek key or fret, the logical ornament of a logical people.

Such arrangements of line form simple linear patterns, and a decorative effect of surface is produced simply by their repetition, especially if the principle of alternation be observed. This principle may be expressed by taking, say, a series of squares or circles, and placing them either in a line as for a border arrangement, or for extension vertically and laterally over a surface, and filling only the alternate square or circle, leaving the alternate ones, or dropping them out altogether (see illustration, p. 111).

[111]

When we desire to go beyond such primitive linear ornaments, however, and introduce natural form, we should still be guided by the same principles, if we desire to produce a strictly decorative effect, while varying them in application to any extent.

It matters not what forms we deal with, floral, animal, human; directly we come to combine them in a design, to control them by a boundary, to [113]inclose them in a space, we shall feel this necessity of controlling line, which, however concealed, is yet essential to bring them into that harmonious relation which is the essence of all design (see illustration, p. 112).

[112]

We may take it as a general rule that the more purely ornamental the purpose of our design, and the more abstract in form it is, the more emphatically we may carry out the principle of correspondence of line between that of the inclosing boundary and that of the design itself; and, *vice versâ,* as the design becomes more pictorial in its appeal and more complex and varied in its elements, the more we may combine the leading motive or principle of line with secondary ones, or with variations, since every fresh element, every new direction of line, every new form introduced, demands some kind of re-echo to bring it into relation with the other elements of the design, or parts of the composition, whatever may be its nature and purpose.

Now, if we seek further the meaning and origin of this necessity of the control of geometric lines and spaces in design, I think we shall find it in the constructive necessities of architecture: for it is certainly from architecture that we derive those typical spaces and panels the designer is so often called upon to fill.

[114]

Origin of Geometric Decorative Spaces

Lintel architecture—the Egyptian and the Greek—gave us the frieze, both continuous, as in that of the Cella of the Parthenon, or divided by triglyphs, which represented the ends of the beams of the primitive timber construction; and the interstices left between these determined the shape of the [115]sculptured panel or slab inserted, and influenced the character of its masses and the lines of its design, which was under the necessity of harmonizing with the whole building (see illustration, p. 114).

The same may be said of the pediments. The angle of the low-pitched roof left another interstice [116]for the sculptor at each end of the building; and I have elsewhere[2] pointed out the influence of the inclosing space and the angles of the pediment of the Parthenon upon the arrangement of the groups within it, and even upon the lines taken by some of the figures, especially the reclining figures near the acute angles.

[2]See "Bases of Design."

Certain lines become inseparably associated with constructive expression, and are used to emphasize it, as the vertical flutings of the Doric column, by repeating the lines of the column itself, emphasize its constructive expression of supporting the weight of the horizontal lintels, the lines of which, repeated in the mouldings of the frieze and cornice, are associated with level restfulness and secure repose.

As examples of design which, while meeting the structural necessities and acknowledging the control of space and general conditions, as the form of the slabs upon which they are sculptured, yet expresses independent movement, the figures of the octagonal tower of the winds at Athens are interesting (see illustration, p. 115).

Quite a different feeling, corresponding to differences in conception and spirit in design, comes in with the Roman round *arch* its allied forms of *spandril* and*vault, lunette* and *medallion,* presenting new spaces for the surface designer, and new suggestions of ornamental line (see illustration, p. 117). It is noticeable how, with the round-arched architecture under Roman, Byzantine (see illustration, p.118), and Renaissance forms, the scroll form of ornament developed, the reason being, I think, that it gave the necessary element of [119]recurring line, whether used in the horizontal frieze in association with round arches, or in spandrils of vaults and arcades, and on marble mosaic pavements.

[117]

[118]

Value of the Recurring Line

The development of Gothic architecture, with its new constructive features and the greater variety of geometric spaces, forms, and interstices which, as a consequence, were available for the designer of associated ornament, whether carved work, mosaic, stained glass, or painting, naturally led to a corresponding variety in invention and decorative adaptation; and we may trace the same principle at work in other forms—I mean the principle of corresponding, counterbalancing, and recurring line—Gothic ornament being indeed generally an essential part of the structure, and architectural features being constantly repeated and utilized for their ornamental value, as in the case of canopies and tabernacle work.

We see, for instance, in the Decorated period the acute gable moulding over the arched recess, niche, doorway, or tomb, lightened and vivified by a floriated finial springing into vigorous curves from a vertical stem, forming an emphatic ogee outline which re-echoes the ogee line of the arch below, and is taken up in variations by the crockets carved upon the sides of the gable; and their spiral ascending lines lead the eye up to the finial which completes the composition. We may trace the same principle in the carved fillings of the subsidiary parts, such as the trefoiled panels, the secondary mouldings, and the cusps of the arches, which continue the line-motive or decorative harmony to the last point (see illustration, p. 120). [120]The elegance and lightness of the pinnacles is increased in the same way, and further emphasized by the long vertical lines of the sunk panels upon their sides.

In church doorways we may see certain voussoirs of the arch allowed to project from the hollow of [121]the concave moulding, and their surfaces carved into bosses of ornament; while, again, the doorway is emphasized by the recurring lines of the mouldings, with their contrasting planes of light and shadow, and the point of their spring is marked [122]by a carved lion, controlled in the design of its contour by the squareness of the block of stone upon which it is carved (see illustration, p. 121).

The carvings of miserere seats in our cathedral choirs often afford instances of ingenious design and arrangement of elements difficult to combine, yet always showing the instinct of following the control of the dominating form and peculiar lines of the seat itself. There is an instance of one from St. David's Cathedral—apparently a humorous satire—a goose-headed woman offering a cake to a man-headed gull (?), or perhaps they are both geese! I won't pretend to say, but it evidently is intended to suggest cupboard love, and there is a portentously large pitcher of ale in reserve on the bench. But note the clever arrangement of the masses and lines, and how the lines of the [123]seat and the curves of the terminating scroll are re-echoed in the lines of the figures and accessories.

A stone-carving from the end of a tomb in the same cathedral—that of Bishop John Morgan, 1504—of a griffin with a shield shows an emphatic repetition of the inclosing line of the arched recess in the curves of the wings which follow it.

There is also a charming corbel of a half-figure of an angel, which, though somewhat defaced, shows the architectural sense very strongly in its design—the vertical droop of the wing-feathers inclosing the figure repeating and continuing the vertical lines of the shafts and the subsidiary mouldings of the arrangement of the drapery, and [124]its termination in crisp foliated forms, which pleasantly counterbalance the set of the scale feathers of the wings and break the semicircular mouldings of the base of the corbel, repeating those of the shafts above.

Adaptability in Design

Adaptation to spaces upon a flat surface is also [125]illustrated in some tile patterns from the same place. They are simple and rude but very effective bits of spacing, and show a thorough grasp of the principles we have been considering—if, indeed, it is so far conscious work at all. But [126]whether or not the outcome of a tradition which seemed to be almost instinctive with mediæval workmen—a tradition which yet left the individual free, and under which design was a thing of life and growth, ever adapting itself to new conditions, and grafting freely new inventions to flower in fresh phantasy upon the ancient stock—the movement in art in the Middle Ages, exhibiting as it does a gradual growth and a constant vitality, always accompanying and adapting itself to structural changes, to life and habit, was really more analogous to the development of mechanical science in our own day, where each new machine is allied to its predecessors, though it supplants them. The one law being adaptability, the one aim to apply means to ends, and more and more perfectly, inessentials and superfluities are shed, and invention triumphs. It is, too, a collective advance, since each engineer, each inventor, builds upon the experience of both his forerunners and his fellow-workers, and everything is brought to an immediately practical test.

We are not yet in the same healthy condition as regards art, and art can never be on the same plane as science, though art may learn much from science, chiefly perhaps in the direction of the inventive adaptation of analogous principles. But in art the question is complicated by human feeling and association, and her strongest appeal is to these, and by these, and as yet we do not seem to have any terms or equivalents precise enough to describe, or any analysis fine enough to discover them.

Extension

The next consideration in spacing we may term [127]*extension*. This bears upon all surface design, but more especially upon the design of patterns intended to repeat over a large surface, and not specially designed for particular spaces. It is a great question whether any design can be entirely satisfactory unless it has been thought out in relation to some particular extent of surface or as adapted to some particular wall or room. Modern industrial conditions preclude this possibility as a rule, and so the only sure ground, beyond individual taste and preference, is technical adaptability to process or material. We should naturally want to give a different character to a textile pattern, whether printed or woven, and intended to hang in folds, from one for flat extension as a wall-paper; and a different character again to such designs intended for extension horizontally from those intended for vertical space alone. Floor patterns, parquets and carpets, for instance, naturally demand different treatment from wall patterns, as those orders of plants in nature which cling and spread on the flat ground differ from those which grow high and maintain themselves in the air, or climb upon trees. The rule of life—*adaptability*—obtains in art as in nature, and, beneath individual preference and passing fashion, works the silent but real law of relation to conditions. This again bears upon the choice of scale, and differentiates the design of dress textiles from furniture textiles, and the design of varied surfaces and objects, which, while demanding their own particular treatment, are brought into general relation by their association with use and the wants of humanity.

[128]

[130]Geometric Structural Plans, etc.

The law governing extension of design over surface is again geometric, and our primal circle and square are again the factors and progenitors of the leading systems which have governed the design of diapers and wall patterns and hangings of all kinds. Nay, the first weaver of the wattled fence discovered the principle of extension in design, and showed its inseparable association with construction; and the builder with brick or stone emphasizes it, producing the elements of linear surface pattern, from the mechanical necessity of the position of the joints of his structure. At a German railway station waiting-room I noticed an effective adaptation of this principle as a wall decoration in two blues upon a stone colour (see illustration, p. 128). We may build upon such emphatic structural lines, either incorporating them with the design motive, as in all rectangular wall diapers, or we may suppress or conceal the actual constructive lines by placing the principal parts or connections of our pattern over them, but one cannot construct a satisfactory pattern to repeat and extend without them; for these constructive lines or plans give the necessary organic life and vigour to such designs, and are as needful to them as the trellis to the tendrils of the vine (see illustration, p. 129).

[129]

The same principle is true of designs upon the curvilinear plan. The mere repetition of the circle by itself gives us a simple geometric pattern, and we are at liberty to emphasize this circular plan as the main motive; or, as in the case of the rectangular plans, to treat it merely as a basis, and develop free scroll motives upon it; or [132]follow it through its principal variations, as in the ogee, formed by dropping out two intermediate semicircles; or the various forms of the scale arrangement. These simple geometric plans are the most generally useful as plans of designs intended for repetition and extension over space, and they are always safe and sound systems to build upon, since a geometric plan is certain to join comfortably if our measurements are right.

[131]

We may, however, often feel that we want something bolder and freer, and start with a motive of sweeping-curves, non-geometric, but even then a certain geometric relation will be necessary, or an equivalent for it, since each curve must be counterbalanced in some way, though not necessarily symmetrically, of course; and even where a square of pattern—say to a wall-paper repeat of twenty-one inches—has been designed, not consciously upon a geometric base, but simply as a composition of lines and masses to repeat, the mechanical conditions of the work when it comes to be printed will supply a certain geometric control, since it necessarily begins in the process of repetition a series of squares of pattern in which the curves are bound to recur in corresponding places. Without a geometric plan of some sort, however, we may easily get into difficulties with awkward leading lines, gaps, or masses, that tumble down, and are only perceived when the paper is printed and hung.

The designer should not feel at all restricted or cramped by his geometric plan, but treat it as an aid and a scaffolding, working in as much variety and richness of detail as he likes, bound only by [133]the necessity of repeating or counterbalancing his forms and lines. In the diagram (p. 131) the plan of making a repeat less obvious by means of what is termed "a drop" is given, and this system also increases the apparent width of a pattern.

Frieze and Field

The feeling which demands some kind of contrast or relief to a field of repeating pattern, however interesting in itself, seems now almost instinctive. It is felt, too, in the case of plain surfaces, where the eye seeks a moulding to give a little variety or pattern-equivalent in play of light and shadow upon different planes, lines, or concavities and convexities. The common plaster cornice placed to unite walls and ceiling, in our ordinary houses, is a concession (on the part even of the jerriest of builders) to the æsthetic sense. We get the decorated frieze in architecture in obedience to the same demand, though originally a necessary feature of lintel construction, as we have seen, from the days of the festal garland hung around the eaves of the classic house, to its perpetuation in stone in so many varieties.[3] The carved garland depending in a series of graceful curves, or contrasted with pendants, or their rhythm punctuated, as it were, by ox-heads, as on the temple of the Sibyls, Tivoli, formed the needed contrast to the plane masonry of the wall below. Sculptured figures, with the added interest of story, as on the choragic monument of Lysicrates, fulfilled the same decorative function in a more complex and elaborate way.

[3]See "Bases of Design."

To satisfy the same feeling we place a frieze [134]above the patterned field of our modern wall-papers. Such a frieze may be considered as a contrasting border to the pattern of the field, much as the border of a carpet, allowing for difference of material and position; or the frieze may assert itself as the dominant decoration of the room. In this case it would be greater in depth than the simpler bordering type. The interest of the field filling would then be subsidiary, and lead up to the frieze. In wall-paper friezes the difficulty in designing is to think of a motive which will not tire the eye in the necessarily frequent repeats of twenty-one inches. Longer ones have occasionally been produced, the limit being sixty inches. It is often a good plan to recur in the main lines or forms of the frieze to some variation of the lines or forms of the field. If, for instance, the main motive in the field was a vertical scroll design, a *horizontal* scroll design upon a large scale used for the frieze would answer, the field being kept flat and quiet; or the fan, or radiating shell form, used as a frieze, above a pattern on the scale plan, would be quite harmonious. Relation and balance of line and mass, and arrangement of quantities in such designs, are the chief considerations.

With painting or modelling an artist is freer, as he is at liberty to design a continuous frieze of figures, and introduce as much variety as he chooses.

A painted frieze of figures above plain oak-panelling has a good effect in a large and well-proportioned room, and is perhaps one of the pleasantest ways of treating interior walls.

[135]

[136]Ceiling Decoration

Ceiling decoration, again, presents problems of extension in designing, and the large flat plaster ceilings of modern rooms are by no means easy to deal with satisfactorily. The simplest way is to resort to wall-paper, and here, restricted in size of repeat and the usual technical requirements of the work, the designer must further consider appropriateness of scale, and position in regard to eye, relation to the wall, and so forth.

The natural demand is for something simpler in treatment than the walls—a re-echo, in some sort, of plans agreeable to the floor, yet with a suggestion of something lighter and freer: here we may safely come back to rectangular and circular plans again for our leading lines and forms.

Painting and modelling, again, offer more elaborate treatment and possibilities, and we know that beautiful works have been done in both ways; but art of this kind seems more appropriate to lofty vaulted chambers and churches, such as one sees in the palaces of Italy, at Genoa and Venice, at Florence and Rome.

I remember a very striking and bold treatment of a flat-beamed ceiling in the Castle of Nuremberg, where a huge black German eagle was painted so as to occupy nearly the whole field of the ceiling, but treated in an extremely flat and heraldic way, the long feathers of the wings following the lines of the beams and falling parallel upon them and between them; and upon the black wings and body of the eagle different shields of arms were displayed in gold and colours, the eagle itself being painted upon the natural unpainted wood—oak, I think. The work belonged [137]to the thirteenth or fourteenth century, I believe. It seemed the very antithesis of Italian finesse and fancy, but the fitness of such decoration entirely depends upon its relation to its surroundings, which in this case were perfectly appropriate.

Co-operative Relation

That is the great point to bear in mind in all design—the sense of relation; nothing stands alone in art. Lines and forms must harmonize with other forms and lines: the elements of any design must meet in friendly co-operation; it is not a blind struggle for existence, a fierce competition, or a strife for ascendency between one motive and another, one form and another, or a war of conflicting efforts. There may be a struggle *outside* the design, in the mind of the designer. He may have tried hard against difficulties to express what he felt, and have only reached harmony through discord and strife, but the work itself should be serene; we should feel that, however various its elements, they are not without their purpose and relation one to another, that all is ordered and organized in harmonious lines, that everything has its use and place, that, in short, it illustrates that excellent motto, whether for art or life: "Each for all, and all for each."

[138]

CHAPTER VI

Of the Fundamental Essentials of Design: Line, Form, Space—Principles of Structural and Ornamental Line in Organic Forms—Form and Mass in Foliage—Roofs—The Mediæval City—Organic and Accidental Beauty—Composition: Formal and Informal—Power of Linear Expression—Relation of Masses and Lines—Principles of Harmonious Composition.

WE may take it, then, from the principles and examples I have endeavoured to put before you in the previous chapters, that there are three fundamental elements or essentials of Design—Line, Form, Space.

Fundamental Essentials of Design

Line we need, not only for our ground-plan and framework, but also to define or express our forms. Form we need to give substance and mass, interest and variety; and it is obvious that Space is required to contain all these elements, while Space asserts its influence, as we have seen, upon both Line and Form in combination upon it, whether object or surface, by the shape of its boundary, the extension of its plane, and the angle and position of its plane in regard to the eye, as well as from the point of view of material and use.

Questions of the character of line and form, and their combination and disposition in or over spaces, are questions of composition. They demand the most careful solution, whatever our subject [139]and purpose may be, from the simplest linear border up to the most elaborate figure design. But although the three essentials to composition must be always present, it is always possible to rely more upon the qualities of one of them for our main motive and interest, keeping the other two subsidiary. We might centralize the chief interest of our composition upon *Line*, for instance, and make harmonious relation or combination of lines our principal object (as in line-design and ornament), or we might rather dwell upon the contours, masses, and contrasts and relationships of*Form*: as in pictorial design, figure compositions of all kinds, and modelling and sculpture: or, again, we might choose that the peculiar character given by the control of certain inclosing spaces should determine the interest of our design, as the due filling of particular panels and geometric shapes; or seek the interest of aerial perspective in the pictorial and atmospheric expression of space.

Taking combinations of Line first, and bearing in mind what has been said regarding its capacities for expression, whether of emotion, direction of force, movement, rest, as well as of facts of structure and surface, let us see if we can trace the principle of harmonious composition, of which these things may be considered as parts.

Line in Organic Forms

Look at any of the systems of line in the organic structures of nature: the radiating ribs of the scallop shell, or the spiral of many other varieties; the set of the feathers upon the expanded wing of a bird; the radiation of the sun's rays; the flowing line of the wave movement; the lines of structure [141]in flowers and leaves; the scales of a fish; the scales of a pine-cone or an artichoke. We feel that any of these combinations of lines are harmonious and beautiful, and we know that they are essential to the character and structure. They are organic lines, in short. They mean life and growth. In principle they are radiating and recurring lines; in each form they repeat each other in varying degrees of direction and declension of curve. No two lines are alike, yet there is no contradiction and no unnecessary line, and variety is combined with unity. Each affords a perfect instance of harmonious composition of line, and gives us definite principles upon which to work (see illustration, p. 140).

[140]

These systems of line in organic nature have been adopted and adapted by art, and are found throughout the historical forms of ornament which, as we have good reason to believe, were often derived from mechanical structures, illustrating the same principles; which, again, the logic of geometry enforces in drawing on plane surfaces.

All organic structures teach us the same lesson of relation and recurrence of line. The bones of all vertebrate animals, from *fish* to *man*, illustrate the constant repetition in different degrees of the same character and direction of line. The vertebral column itself is an instance, and the recurring spring of the ribs from it, like the branches from the stem of a tree, further expressed in the ramification of the jointed bones of the limbs and extremities. The principle may be followed out in the structure of the muscles in their radiating fibres, which the delicate contours and flowing lines of [144]the surface of the body only combine in a greater degree of subtlety (see illustration, p. 142).

[142]

Look at the anatomy of any tree, as it is disclosed to us in its wintry leaflessness, a beautiful composition of line rather than of form (see illustration, p. 143).

[143]

Here we see organic life and structure expressed in the vigorous spring of inter-dependent and corresponding curves, from the rigid sinuous column of the main stem springing from the ground, presently divided into the main forks of the branches, which again subdivide and subdivide into smaller forks, so that the tree may sustain and spread its life in the air and the sun, both supporting and continuing its existence by this wonderful economic system of co-operative, subdivided, and graduated helpfulness.

The massive green pavilion of summer, which this delicate vaulting of branch-work sustains, gives us another, more sumptuous, but perhaps not a greater beauty in the combination or substitution of form and mass for line composition.

Form and Mass in Foliage

We might express, in an abstract way, the principle of the line-structure of the ramifying tree by super-imposing vertically fork upon fork in gradually diminishing scale, either curvilinear or rectangular; and the principle of the mass-structure in the formation of the foliage might be expressed by a series of overlapping curves, suggestive of scales or cloud masses: to both of which indeed they correspond in principle, illustrating the scale principle in detail and the cloud principle in the mass; thus repeating the same general law of [146]natural roofing, or covering, in different materials (see illustration, p. 145).

[145]

In a mass of foliage each leaf falls partly over the one below it, as by the system of their growth and suspension upon the stem they are of course bound to do, whether symmetric or alternate in their arrangement, the gaps caused by decay or accident being generally filled by new shoots. Each shoot, eager to expand its leaves in the light, ever spreading, forms mass after mass of the beautiful green panoply—the coat armour of the forest, arboreal man's first form of domestic architecture.

The principle of structure here is just the same as the overlapping principle of the tiles and slates upon our ordinary house-roofs; but each leafy tile is different, being alive, and in the mass infinitely varied and beautiful in form and colour, instead of being mechanical and uniform, as we try to make our artificial roofs.

German Roofs

Very pretty and varied effects are produced in [147]the old roofs of southern Germany by the use of different coloured glazed tiles—red, green, and yellow—arranged in simple patterns. One of the old towers at Lindau has such a roof, and the colour effect is very rich and striking.

But I must not be led into a disquisition upon roofs further than in so far as they illustrate the subject of composition of line and form, and from [148]the painter's point of view they frequently do in a very delightful and instructive way.

What, for instance, can be more varied and charming than the compositions we constantly meet with in the rich backgrounds of Albert Dürer? Those steep barn roofs, and those quaint German towns inclosed in walls with protecting towers—nests of steep tiled gables of every imaginable degree—which give so much character and interest to his designs, as in the background of his copper-plates "The Prodigal Son" and "St. Anthony" here given. Their prototypes still exist here and there in Germany, in such towns as Rothenburg, practically unchanged since the sixteenth century, and give one an excellent idea of what such houses were like. A visit there is like a leap back into the Middle Ages. Every street is a varied and interesting composition. No two houses are alike. They were built by the citizens to really pass their lives in. The town is strongly placed upon the crest of a hill, with a river at its foot, and well fortified and protected by massive encircling walls and towers and deep gates, which give it so strong and picturesque a character, while the timber and tile-roofed gallery for the warders still exists along the inside of the walls. Such cities arose by the strength of the social bond among men—the necessity for mutual help in the maintenance of a higher standard of life, and mutual protection against the ravages of sinister powers.

The Mediæval City

Strong externally, internally they were made as home-like and full of the varied delight of the eyes, as if the people had reasoned, "Since we must live close together in a small place, let us make it as[149]delightful and romantic as we can." We know that the idea of Paradise and the New Jerusalem to the imagination of the Middle Ages was always [150]the fair walled garden and the fenced city. The painters embodied the idea of security and protection from the savage and destructive forces of nature and man—a sanctuary of peace, a garden of delight.

We have in modern times turned rather from the city as a complete and beautiful thing, to the individual home, and to the interior of that, and, in the modern competitive search for the necessary straws and sticks to make our individualist-domestic composition of comfort and artistic completeness, bowers are too often built upon the ruins of others, or are fair by reason of surrounding degradation. The common collective comfort and delight of the eyes is too often ignored, so that it comes about that, if our modern cities possess any elements of beauty or picturesqueness, it is rather owing to accidents and to the transfiguring effects of atmosphere than to the beauty or variety of architectural form and colour. We have to seek inspiration among the fragments of the dead past in monuments and art schools.

Organic and Accidental Beauty

The modern development of the municipality and extension of its functions may, indeed, do something, as it has done, and is doing, something to protect public health and further public education; but we have yet to wait for the full results, and everything must finally depend upon the public spirit and disinterestedness of the citizens, and in matters of art upon a very decided but somewhat rare and peculiar sympathy and taste, as well as enthusiasm.

The absence of beauty of line, form, and proportion from the external aspects of daily life in towns has probably a greater effect than we are apt to [151]realize in deadening the imagination, and it certainly seems to produce a certain insensibility to beauty of line and composition, since the perception must necessarily be blunted by being inured to the commonplace and sordid. The instinct for harmony of line and form becomes weakened, and can only be slowly revived by long and careful study in art, instead of finding its constant and most vital stimulus in every street.

For all that, however, an eye trained to observe and select may, even in the dullest and dingiest street, find artistic suggestions, if not in the buildings, then in the life. And where there is life, movement, humanity, there is sure to be character and interest. Groups of children playing will give us plenty of suggestions for figure composition. Workpeople going to and from their work, the common works going on in the street, the waggons and horses, the shoal of faces, the ceaseless stream of life—all these things, whether we are able to reproduce them as direct illustrations of the life of our time, or are moved only to select from them vivid suggestions to give force to ideal conceptions, should all be noted—photographed, as it were, instantaneously upon the sensitive plate of the mind's vision. We can only learn the laws of movement by observing movement—the swing and poise of the figure, the relation of the lines of limbs and drapery to the direction of force and centre of gravity, so important in composition. We must constantly supplement our school and studio work by these direct impressions of vivid life and movement, and neglect no opportunity or despise no source or suggestion.

[152]There are still in England to be found such old-world corners as the quaint street of Canterbury (p. 153), which forms an excellent study in the composition of angular and vertical lines.

[153]

Formal Composition

We may perceive that there are at least two kinds of composition, which may be distinguished as:

I. Formal.

II. Informal.

I. Under the head of Formal may be classed all those systems of structural line with which I started, and which are found either as leading motives or fundamental plans and bases throughout ornamental design. Yet even these may be used in composition of figures and other forms where the object is more or less formal and decorative, as governing plans or controlling lines.

The radiating ribs of a fan, for instance, might be utilized as the natural boundaries and inclosing lines of a series of vertical figures following the radiating lines. A strictly logical design of the kind would be a series of figures with uplifted arms, forming radiating lines from the shoulders, somewhat in the position of Blake's well-known and beautiful composition of the Morning Stars in the Book of Job, already illustrated.

Using the overlapping vertical scale plan we should get relative positions for a formal composition of three figures, although they need not necessarily be formal in detail. A typical design of three associated ideas treated emblematically would be the most natural use of such an arrangement—as Faith, Hope, and Charity; Liberty, Equality, Fraternity; Science, Art, and Industry; [154]or the three goddesses Heré, Pallas, and Aphrodite, as choice and purpose might decide. A semicircular scale plan would not only repeat in a safe and sound manner, but would afford suggestive shapes in which to throw designs of figures, and could be effectively utilized either for a wall or ceiling repeat.

The inclosure formed by two spiral lines gives a graceful ornamental shape for a half-reclining figure; while a series of floating or flying figures linking their hands would be appropriately governed by similar spiral lines, uniting them with the meandering wave line (see illustration, p. 155).

[155]

Upon a series of semicircles or ellipses, alternating horizontally, might be arranged a little frieze of children with skipping ropes, or Amorini with pendent garlands; the up-and-down movement in the former case being conveyed by a variation, each alternate semicircle being struck upwards. This would restore the emphatic wave or spiral line, which always conveys the sense of rhythmic movement in a design.

Such a line, vertically employed, will give again a good plan for a series of seated figures, say emblematic of the Hours, where similarity of attitude and type would be appropriate, while the emblems and accessories might be varied. A severer treatment would be suggested by making the controlling line angular (see illustration, p. 156).

[156]

Such are a few illustrations of what I have termed formal composition, in which the geometric and structural plans of pure ornament or ornamental line maybe utilized to combine, control, or even suggest figure designs.

[157]Informal Composition

II. While formal compositions, though naturally falling into classes and types, may be varied to a very great extent, when we come to informal compositions the variations are unlimited, and a vista of extraordinary and apparently endless choice, invention, and selection opens out before the designer, co-extensive with the variety of nature herself.

In seeking harmonious and expressive composition in the pictorial direction the guides are much less definite and secure. Individual feeling and instinct, which must have an important influence in all kinds of designing, are in this direction paramount. Yet even here, if we look beneath the apparent freedom and informality, we find certain laws at work which seem to differ only in degree from the more definite and constructive control of line which we have been considering. In the first place, there are our direct impressions from nature; and, secondly, our conscious aims and efforts to express an idea in our minds. We have the same restricted and definite forms of language and materials in each case—line, form, space, brushes, pencil, colour, paper, canvas, or clay. We are taken by some particular scene: the composition of line and form at a particular spot attracts us more than another. We do not stop as a rule to ask why, since it usually takes all our time and our best skill to get into shape what we are seeking—and carry away with us an artistic record of the place. We have seen that in the case of certain natural structures, shells, leaves, flowers, the fundamental structural lines are so beautiful that they not only form ornament in themselves,[158]but furnish the basis for whole types and families of ornament. When we look at a landscape, putting aside for the moment all the surface charms of colour and effect, and concentrating our attention upon its lines of structures, we shall find that it owes a great part of its beauty to the harmonious relation of its leading lines, or to certain pleasant contrasts, or a certain impressiveness of form and mass, and at the same time we shall perceive that this linear expression is inseparable from the sentiment or emotion suggested by that particular scene.

A gentle southern landscape—undulating downs, and wandering sheep-walks; the soft rounded masses of the sheep upon smooth cropped turf—all these are so many notes or words in the language of line and form which go to express the idea of pastoral life. They are inextricably bound up with inseparable associations conveyed by such lines and forms. The undulating lines of resting or dancing figures would only give point, true emphasis, and variety, and a note of contrast in the forms would serve to bring out the general sentiment more strongly.

Substitute rugged rocks, swollen torrents, wind-tossed trees and stormy skies, and all is changed. Such things cannot be expressed without much more emphatic lines and masses, and the use of opposing angles and energetic curves of movement which would be destructive of the sentiment of peace, in other cases. Yet even then to convey the expression of energy and rapid movement, concerted groups of lines are none the less necessary (see illustration, p. 159).

[159]

[160]Such comparisons indicate not only that there is a necessary association of ideas with certain lines and forms, but also that certain relations and associations of line of a similar character are necessary to produce a harmonious composition, and one which conveys a definite and pervading sentiment or emotion, just as we saw that the controlling lines of structural curves, spirals, and angles require to be in relation, and to be re-echoed by the character of the design they inclose or which is built upon them.

The same law holds true in figure composition. The sense of repose and restfulness necessary to sitting or reclining groups depends upon the gentle declivities of the curves and their gradual descent to the horizontal.

[161]

Draw a figure sitting rigid, tense, and alert, and you destroy the sense of repose at once, and you are obliged also to resort to angles, still more emphatic where strong action is to be expressed; while to express continual or progressive movement, a choice of associated lines of action in different stages of progress leading up to the crescendo of the final one (as in a group of mowers) would be necessary (see illustrations, p. 161). We cannot, then, in any composition have too definite a conception. We must, at any sacrifice of detail, bring out the main expression and meaning. Every group of figures must be in the strictest relation to each other and to the central interest or expression of the design. You cannot, for instance, in a procession of figures, make your faces turn all sorts of ways without stopping the onward movement which is essential to the idea of a [162]procession. This would not preclude variety, but the general tendency must be in one direction. Every line in a composition must lead up to the central idea, and be subordinated or contributory to it (see illustration, Nos. 1 and 2, p. 163).

[163]

The same with masses: you cannot put a number of forms together without some sort of relation, either of general character and contour or some uniting line. We may learn this principle from nature also. Look at a heap of broken stones and débris, which in detail may contain all sorts of varieties of form, as we find them tumbled down a steep place, as the rocky bed of a mountain stream, a heap of boulders upon a hillside, or the débris from a quarry or mine; in each case the law of gravity and the persistence of force working together arrange the diverse forms in masses controlled by the lines, which express the direction and degree of descent, and the pressure of force. The same thing may be seen on any hilly ground after heavy rain; the scattered pebbles are arranged in related groups, combined and composed by the flow of miniature streams, which channel the face of the ground and form hollows for their reception (see Nos. 3 and 4, p.163). The force of the tides and currents upon the sea-shore illustrates the same principle and affords us magnificent lessons in composition, not only in the delicate lines taken by the sculptured sand, but in the harmonious grouping of masses of shingle and shells, weeds and drift, arranged by the movement of the waves.

Principles of Harmonious Composition

So that we may see that the principles of harmonious composition are not the outcome of merely [164]capricious fancy or pedantic rule, but are illustrated throughout the visible world by the laws and forces of the material universe. It is for the artist to observe and apply them in his own work of re-creation.

[165]

CHAPTER VII

Of the Relief of Form—Three Methods—Contrast—Light and Shade, and Modelling—The Use of Contrast and Planes in Pattern Designing—Decorative Relief—Simple Linear Contrast—Relief by Linear Shading—Different Emphasis in relieving Form by Shading Lines—Relief by means of Light and Shade alone without Outline—Photographic Projection—Relief by different Planes and Contrasts of Concave and Convex Surfaces in Architectural Mouldings—Modelled Relief—Decorative Use of Light and Shade, and different Planes in Modelling and Carving—Egyptian System of Relief Sculpture—Greek and Gothic Architectural Sculpture, influenced by Structural and Ornamental Feeling—Sculptural Tombs, Medals, Coins, Gems—Florentine Fifteenth-century Reliefs—Desideriodi Settignano.

WE come now to the consideration of the various means and methods of expressing relief in line and form.

We may define a form in outline and give it different qualities of expression by altering the quality and consistency of our outline, and we may obtain very different kinds of decorative effect by the use of lines of various degrees of thickness or thinness; but if we want to give it force and colour, and to distinguish it from its background more emphatically, we must add to our outline.

Three Methods of Expressing Relief

There are three principal methods or systems of giving relief by adding to our outline.

One is the method of giving relief to form by contrasts of tone, colour, or tint.

[166]Another by means of the expression of light and shade: and the third by means of modelling in relief.

Now, still keeping to expression by means of line, the three arms I have sketched (p. 167) illustrate: (1) the form in outline alone; (2) the contrast method; and (3) the light and shade method. The three pots underneath illustrate the same three stages in a simpler manner.

In number one we see the outline defining the form pure and simple: in number two the form is relieved by a half-tone formed of diagonal lines, forming a plane or background behind it. The arm is still further relieved by the dark drapery. Number three shows the relief carried further by lines expressive of the modelling of the arm and the rounding of the pot, and also by cast shadows from the forms.

[167]

The system of expressing relief I have termed relief by contrast includes two kinds of contrast: there are the contrasts of line and form, and there are the contrasts of planes of tone or tint and local colour. We may consider that the contrast method covers generally all forms of pattern and certain kinds of pictorial design. The method of expressing relief by means of line covers generally all forms of design in black and white, graphic sketching, pen-drawing, and work with the point of all kinds.

Of the Use of Contrast and Planes

Taking the principle of contrast as applied to pattern design, we can, even within the limited range of black and white and half-tint (as expressed by lines), get a considerable amount of decorative effect. In the first place by bringing out our pattern, [168]previously outlined, upon a black ground (as in Nos. 1 and 2, p. 169), increasing the richness of effect, and getting a second plane by treating the lower part in an open tint of line.

Simple contrasts of dark upon light or light upon dark are effective, and sufficient for many purposes, such as borders (as in Nos. 2 and 3, p. 169).

When a lighter kind of relief and effect is required, the recurring forms in a border are often sufficiently emphasized by a tint of open lines: movement and variety being given by making them follow the minor curves of the successive forms, as in this instance (No 4, p. 169) the movement of the water is suggested behind the fish.

The relation of the plain ground-work to the figure of the pattern is also an important point; indeed the plain parts of the pattern, or the interstices and intervals of the pattern, are as essential to the pattern as the figured parts.

In designs intended for various processes of manufacture, such as printed or woven textiles, wall-papers, etc., where blocks or rollers are used to repeat the pattern, the extent of plain in proportion to figured parts must be governed in some measure by the practicable size of the repeat: but within certain limits great variety of proportion is possible.

A simple but essentially decorative principle is to preserve a certain equality between the figured masses and the ground masses. The leaf patterns (Nos. 6 and 7, p. 169) consist simply of the repetition and reversal of a single element. An emphatic effect is obtained by bringing the leaves out black upon a white ground (as in No. 6), while a flatter [170]and softer effect is the result of throwing them upon a plane of half-tint expressed by horizontal lines, with a similar effect of relief to that which would be given by the warp, if the pattern were woven.

For larger surfaces, greater repose and dignity in pattern may be obtained by a greater proportion of the repeat being occupied by the ground (as in No. 5, p.169).

[169]

Indeed we may consider as a general principle that the larger the interspaces of the ground, plane, or field of the pattern, the lighter in tint they should be, or the necessary flatness is apt to be lost. Relief in pattern design may be said to be adding interest and richness without losing the flatness and repose of the design as a whole. When pattern and ground are fairly equally balanced in quantity the ground may be rich and dark, and darkest as the interstices, where the ground is shown, become less. The figure of a pattern relieved as light upon a dark plane, as a rule, requires to be fuller in form than dark-figuring upon a light ground.

Decorative Relief

In decorative work the use of contrast in the relief of parts of a design is often useful and effective, as, for instance, the dark shading or treatment in black or flat tone of the alternating under side of a turn-over leaf border.

The decorative value of this principle is recognized by heraldic designers in the treatment of the mantling of the helmet, which in earlier times is treated simply as a hanging or flying strip of drapery with a lining of a different colour, by which it is relieved as it hangs in simple spiral folds. This ornamental element became developed by the [171]designers of the fifteenth and sixteenth centuries into elaborate scroll designs springing from the circlet of the helmet and surrounding the shield: but the principle of the turned-up lining remained, often variegated and enriched with heraldic patterns (see illustrations, pp. 172, 173).[4]

[4]The increased importance given to the mantling in later times may have been due to the disappearance of the housings of the knight's horse and his surcoat, which originally displayed his arms and colours. The mantling of later times displayed the heraldic colours of the knight, when, being clad in plate armour, there was no other means of displaying them except on the shield. Decoratively, of course, the mantling is of great value to the heraldic designer, enabling him to form much more graceful compositions, to combine diverse and rigid elements with free and flowing lines and masses, and to fill panels with greater richness and effect, whether carved or painted, or both.

[172]

[173]

Use of Diapered Backgrounds

The principle, too, of counterchange in heraldry answers to our principle of relief by contrast, and though its chief charm lies in its ornamental range of form and colour combinations, it can be expressed in black and white, and it remains a universal principle throughout decorative art. The decorative effect and charm of the relief of large and bold forms upon rich and delicate diapers is also an important resource of the designer. The monumental art of the Middle Ages affords multitudes of examples of this principle in ornamental treatment. The miniaturist of the twelfth and thirteenth centuries constantly relieved his groups of figures upon a diapered ground. The architectural sculptor relieved the broad masses of flowing drapery and the bold projection of his effigies and recumbent figures by delicately chiselled diapers upon the surface of the wall behind them. This treatment [174]may frequently be seen in the recessed tombs of the fourteenth century.

The incisor of memorial brasses, again, more especially in continental examples, shows a fondness for the same principle. The long vertical lines of drapery of ladies and ecclesiastics, the broad masses of the heraldic surcoat, or armour of the knights, the rich and heavy furred gowns of the burghers, are often relieved upon beautiful diapered or arabesque grounds, generally embodying some heraldic device, motto, or emblem of the person or family whose tomb it ornaments. Such decoration is strictly linear, yet within its own limits, and perhaps because of them, we find in this province of design extremely admirable work, no less for delineation of character and decorative treatment than for ornamental invention controlled by strict economy of line.

[175]

Relief of Form by Linear Shading

This brings us to the consideration of our second method of relief by means of line.

Take any simple allied elements to form a repeating pattern, say spiral shells, place them at certain rhythmic intervals, and we can unite and at the same time give them relief by filling in the ground by a series of waved lines to suggest the ribbed sand. Add a few dots to soften and vary the effect, and we get a pattern of a certain balance and consistency (No. 1, p. 177).

[177]

With the more varied and complex floral form, but treated in a very abstract way, placing the daisies in a line, horizontally, and reversing the sprig for the alternate row, we have another motive, which is connected and steadied as well as relieved by the suggestion of grass blades in [176]groups of three slightly radiated vertical strokes (No. 2, p. 177). A pattern of two elements, again, may be formed in a still more simple way by linear contrast, as in No. 3, where the pyramidal trees are formed by a continuous serpentine stroke of the pen terminating in a spiral stem. The diagonal arrangement of the trees produces a chequer, the intervals of which can be varied by the contrasting black masses of the birds.

In graphic drawing, lines to express forms in the relief of light and shade are often needed to give additional force even where no great degree of realism is desired. A tint formed by horizontal lines is sufficient to relieve a face from the background and give it solidity, while local colour may be given to the hair, and at the same time serve to relieve the leaves of a wreath encircling the head (see illustration, p. 178).

The rich effect of clustered apples growing among their leaves could hardly be suggested without the use of lines expressive of light and shade, the interstices of the deepest shade running into solid black (p. 178). In adding lines in this kind of way to give relief or extra richness or force, the draughtsman is really designing a system of lines upon his outline basis, which may have quite as decorative a quality as the outline itself. At the same time nothing is more characteristic of the artist than the way in which such lines are used, and of course the choice of direction and arrangement of such lines will make all the difference in the effect of the drawing.

Diagonal Shading

Where the object is to express the figure in broad masses of light and shade, the use of a [178]series of diagonal lines is an effective, and probably the most ready and rapid, method when working with the pen (see p. 179). This system of expressing the broad surfaces of shade was much used by the Italian masters of the Renaissance [180]in their rapid pen sketches and studies of figures, and a certain breadth and style is given to their drawings owing in part to the simplicity of this linear treatment.

[179]

Emphasis

No doubt the simpler the system of line adopted in giving relief to figures the better, if the particular expression aimed at is accomplished, and, as a general rule, we should endeavour to get the necessary force and depth without the use of cross-line, or many different directions of line in shading a figure: but, given any power of draughtsmanship, the individuality of the artist is bound to come in, and it is not likely, nor is it to be desired, that any two artists in line should give exactly the same account of natural fact, or reproduce the images in their minds in the same forms, any more than we should expect two writers to express their ideas in the same terms.

The kind and degree of emphasis upon different parts, the selection of moment or fact, would all naturally make considerable differences in the treatment. The three sketches of the skirt dancer are given as instances of the different effects and expression to be obtained in rendering the same subject (p. 181).

[181]

In A the broad relief of the white dress against the tones of the floor and background, and the darker note of the hair, are the facts chiefly dwelt upon. In Bthe form of the figure is brought out in broad light and shade and cast shadow, and the dress relieved by radiating folds. In C quicker movement is given, the lines of the successive wave-shaped folds radiating spirally from the shoulders being the chief means of conveying this, [182]while the head and arms are thrown into strong relief against a dark background, the cast shadow being of a lighter tone.

The direction of line used in relieving forms, and expressing modelling and details, must depend much upon individual taste and feeling as well as knowledge of form. The element of beauty of design also comes in, and the question between this and force or literalness—the difference between a study or direct transcript from nature, and a design with a purely ornamental aim, or a composition directed mainly to the expression of a particular idea or emotion.

Such considerations will ultimately determine the choice and use of line, the degree of relief and emphasis, for these and the direction of the line itself are the syllables and the words which will convey the purport of the work to the mind of the beholder.

Study of the masters of line—Dürer, Titian, Mantegna, Holbein—will inform us as to its capacities and limitations. The limitations, too, of method and material will be a powerful factor in the determination of style in the use of line and in the economy of its use.

The bold firm line suitable to the facsimile woodcut, the broad and simple treatment of line with solid black useful in the plank-cut line block to be used with colour blocks, the comparatively free and unconditioned pen-drawing for the surface-printed process block—all these will finally give a certain character to our work beyond our own idiosyncrasies in the use of the pen or the brush.

[183]

[184]Useful things may be learned by the way, such as Albert Dürer's principle of giving substance to his figures and details, more especially seen in his treatment of drapery, when the lines run into solid black and express the deeper folds and give emphasis and solidity to the figure (p. 183). The reproductions here given of sketches of drapery by Filippino Lippi and Raphael also show the same principle.

A figure or object of any kind, seen in full light and shade, is relieved at any of its edges either as dark against light, or as light against dark, and we recognize it as a solid form in this way; the boundaries of natural light and shade defining it, and projecting it from the background upon the vision. There may be infinite modulations, of course, [186]between the light part, the half-tones, and the darkest parts; but this broad principle governs all work representing light and shade.

[185]

It is, in fact, *the principle of the relief of form* represented upon a plane surface.

[187]Relief by Light and Shade Alone

If the draughtsman's object be to represent the *appearance* of a figure or any object in full natural light and shade with the pen or other point, he could do so without using outline at all, but by simply observing this principle and defining the boundaries of light on dark or half-tone in their proper masses and relations. The pen sketch of the man with the hoe (p.188) is intended to illustrate this method.

[188]

There is also the method of representing form in relief by means of working with white line only upon a dark ground, the modelling and planes of surface being entirely expressed in this way (as in A, p. 189). This may be termed drawing by means of *light*, and may be contrasted with the opposite method of working by means of black line only on a light ground, or drawing by means of*shade* (as in B, p. 189).

[189]

Yet another method, and one in which the effect of relief can be obtained more readily and rapidly, perhaps, is by working on a half-toned paper, drawing in the form with pencil, chalk, or brush, blocking in the darker shadows and heightening the highest lights with touches of white. These white touches, however, should be strictly limited to the highest lights. This method is represented by the half-tone blocks used in this book, those which were taken from drawings made on brown paper and touched with white.

The Principle of the Photograph

The definition of form by means of light is strictly the principle of the photograph, which comprehends and illustrates its complementary of relief by means of shade, and I think it is due to the influence of the photograph that modern black-and-white artists [190]have so often worked on these principles. The drawings of Frederick Walker and Charles Keene may be referred to as examples. I shall, however, hope to return to this branch of the subject later.

Relief in Architectural Mouldings

So far we have been considering the relief of form by means of line. We now come to what may be termed the relief of form by actual form and plane, or modelling in actual light and shade, as in architecture and sculptors' and carvers' work. Then relief is gained by the contrast of actually different planes, forms, surfaces, and textures. The simplest illustrations of the principles of modelled relief are to be found in architectural mouldings, by means of which buildings are relieved and enriched, and important structural or functional parts are emphasized, as in cornices and ribs of vaults, arches, and openings.

Place a concave moulding side by side with a convex one either horizontally or vertically, and a certain pleasant effect of contrasting light and shade is the result, reminding one of the recurring concave and convex of the rolling waves of the sea (A, p. 191).

A series of flat planes of different widths and at different levels also produces a pleasant kind of relief useful in a picture frame or the jamb of a door (B).

All architectural mouldings might be said to be modifications or combinations of the principles illustrated by these two.

Very different feeling may be expressed in mouldings, and if we compare the two types, the classical and the Gothic, the comparatively broad and simple effect of the former (C, D, E, F, G) [192]contrasts with the richness and variety and the stronger effect of light and shade, produced by deep undercutting, in the latter (H, I, J, K).

[191]

The Romans, however, produced rich and highly ornate effects in the use of these types of mouldings, as they reappeared in the Corinthian order, the ovolo cut into the egg and dart, with the Astralagus beneath, the Cyma recta above the brackets of the cornice casting a bold shadow, and both in the cornice and the hollow beneath the dentils enriched with carving, as seen in the splendid fragment of the Forum of Nerva.

[193]

When we pass to the more complex problems of figure modelling and sculpture, it is but carrying on and developing the same principle of the contrast of planes, of the relief of plane upon plane, of forms upon one plane, to forms upon forms in many planes. From the contrast of bead and hollow we come to consider the contrast between the rounded limb and the sinuous folds of drapery; from the rhythm of the acanthus scroll we turn to the less obvious but none the less existing rhythm of the sculptural frieze.

Line, we may say, controls the modeller's and sculptor's composition, but form and its treatment in light and shade give him his means of ornament. The delicate contours of faces and limbs contrasted with the spiral and radiating folds of drapery, or rich clusters of leaves and fruits, the forms of animals and the wings of birds—these are his decorative resources.

Egyptian Reliefs

The early stages of sculpture in relief may be seen in the monumental work of ancient Egypt.

Simple incised work appears to have been the [194]first stage, and the forms afterwards slightly modelled or rounded at the edges into the hollow of the sunk outline.

Large figures and tables of hieroglyphic inscription were thus cut upon vast mural surfaces, and carried across the joints of the masonry, without disturbing the flatness and repose of the wall surface (p. 195). The Egyptians, indeed, seem to have treated their walls more as if they were books for record and statement, symbol and hieroglyphic.

[195]

Messrs. Perrot and Chipiez, in their "History of Ancient Art in Egypt," speak of three processes in the treatment of Egyptian reliefs (vol. ii., p. 284):

1. That followed by the Greeks, in which the figures are left standing out from a smooth bed, sometimes slightly hollowed near the contours (see illustration, p. 196).
2. Where the figures are modelled in relief in a sunk hollow, from an inch to one and a half inch deep.
3. Where the surface of the figures and the bed or field of relief are kept on one level (see illustration, p. 196), the contours indicated by hollow lines cut into the stone; very little modelling, little more than silhouette, in which the outline is shown by a hollow instead of by the stroke of a pencil or brush.

One would be inclined to reverse the order of these three processes, on the supposition that No. 3 was the earliest process, and that it arose, as I have conjectured, from the practice of representing forms by incised lines only.

There is certainly a strong family likeness as to [197]method between the Egyptian reliefs and the Assyrian, the Persian, and the archaic Greek; and there is a far greater difference in treatment between archaic Greek relief sculpture and the work of the Phidian period than between the archaic work of the three races named.

The strictly mural and decorative conditions which governed ancient sculpture no doubt gave to Greek sculpture in its perfection a certain dignity, simplicity, and restraint, and also accounted in a great measure for that rhythmic control of invisible structural and ornamental line which asserts itself in such works as the Pan-Athenaic frieze. It was strictly slab sculpture, and became part of the surface of the wall.

[196]

Gothic Sculpture

The structural and ornamental feeling also asserts itself strongly in Gothic sculpture, owing to its close association with architecture, as, when it was not an integral part of the structure, it was always an essential part of the expression of the building, and it was this which controlled its treatment decoratively, in its scale and its system and degree of relief.

In the porches of the Gallo-Roman churches of France of the twelfth century, the figures occupying the place of shafts became columnar in treatment, the sinuous formalized draperies wrapped around the elongated figures, or falling in vertical folds, as in the figures in the western door of Chartres Cathedral (p. 199). The lines of the design of the sculptured tympanum were strictly related to the space, and the degree and treatment of the relief clearly felt in regard to the architectural effect (p. 201).

[199]

[201]

[198]Architectural Influence

In the sculptured tombs of the Middle Ages, with their recumbent figures and heraldic enrichments, again, we see this architectonic sense influencing the treatment of form and relief, as these monuments were strictly architectural decorations, often incorporating its forms and details, and often built into the structure of the church or cathedral itself, as in the case of the recessed and canopied tombs of the thirteenth and fourteenth centuries.

As sculptures became detached from the building and wall, and appeared in full relief in the round, though still, as it were, carrying a reminiscence of their origin with them in the shape of the moulded pedestal, architectural control became less and less felt, statues in consequence being less and less related to their surroundings. The individual feeling of the sculptor or the traditions of his school and training alone influenced his treatment, until we get the incidental and dramatic or sentimental isolated figure or group of modern days.

Medals and Coins

It is noteworthy, however, that even in the smaller works of the modeller, carver, or sculptor of the Middle Ages or the early Renaissance, a sense of decorative fitness and structural sense is always present. We see it in the carved ornaments of seats and furniture, in the design and treatment of coins and seals and gems and medals. These latter from the time of the ancient Greeks afford beautiful examples of the decorative treatment of relief in strict relation to the object and purpose. The skill and taste of the Greeks seemed to have been largely inherited by the artists of the earlier Italian Renaissance, such as Pisano, whose famous medal of the Malatesta of Rimini affords a splendid [200]instance not only of the treatment of the portrait and subject on the reverse perfectly adapted to its method and purpose, but also of the artistic use of lettering as a decorative feature (see p. 203).

[203]

The treatment and relief of figures and heads upon the plane surfaces of metals and coins, the composition controlled by the circular form, have always been a fine test of both modelling and decorative skill and taste. Breadth is given by a flatness in the treatment of successive planes of low relief, which rise to their highest projection from the ground, in the case of a head in profile, about its centre. The delicate perception of the relation of the planes of surface is important, as well as the decorative effect to be obtained by arrangement of the light and shade masses and the contrast of textures, such as hair and the folds of drapery, to the smooth contours of faces and figures, and the rectangular forms of lettering.

In gems we see the use made of the concave ground, which gives an effective relief to the figure design in convex upon it. Bolder projection of prominent parts are here necessary in contrast to the retiring planes, the work being on so small a scale, and also in view of its seal-like character; for, of course, it is the method of producing form by incision, and modelling by cutting and hollowing out, that gives the peculiar character to gems and seals; and it is in forming human figures that the building up of the form by a series of ovals, spoken of in a previous chapter, becomes really of practical value: the method of hollowing the stone or metal in cutting the gem or making a [202]die and the character of the tool leading naturally in that direction.

Desiderio di Settignano

Perhaps the most delicate and beautiful kind of sculptured or modelled relief is to be found in the work of the Florentine school of the fifteenth century, more especially that of Donatello and Desiderio di Settignano, who seem indeed to have caught the feeling and spirit of the best Greek period, with fresh inspiration and suggestion from nature and the life around them, as well as an added charm of grace and sweetness.

It is difficult to imagine that marble carving in low relief can be carried to greater perfection than it is in the well-known small relief by Desiderio di Settignano of the "Madonna and Child," now in the Italian Court of the South Kensington Museum. The delicate yet firmly chiselled faces and hands, the smooth surfaces of the flesh, and the folds of drapery, emerging from, or sinking into, the varied planes of the ground, for refinement of feeling and treatment seem almost akin to the art of the painter in the tenderness of their expression.

[204]

CHAPTER VIII

Of the Expression of Relief in Line-drawing—Graphic Aim and Ornamental Aim—Superficial Appearance and Constructive Reality—Accidents and Essentials—Representation and Suggestion of Natural Form in Design—The Outward Vision and the Inner Vision.

I HAVE already said that when we add lines or tints of shadow, local colour or surface, to an outline drawing, we are seeking to express form in a more complete way than can be done in outline alone. These added lines or tints give what we call relief. That is their purpose and function, whether by that added relief we wish to produce an ornamental effect or simply to approach nearer to the full relief of nature, for of course the degrees of relief are many.

Relief in Line-Drawing

What may be called the natural principle of relief—that system of light and shade by which a figure or any solid object is perceived as such by the eye—consists in each part of the form being thrown into more or less contrast by appearing as dark on light upon its background, more especially at its edges. A figure wholly dark, say in black drapery, appearing against a light ground, might be supposed to be flat if no cast shadow was seen; the same with the reverse—a light figure upon a dark ground—except that in this latter [205]case, unless the light was very level and flat, a certain concentration of light upon the highest parts, or indicating a modulation of shadow in interstices, might betray its solidity (see p. 206).

But if we place a figure so that the light falls from one side, we perceive that it at once stands out in bold relief in broad planes of light and shade, further emphasized by cast shadows (p. 207).

It would be possible to represent or to express a figure or object so lighted by means of laying in the modulations and planes of shadow only, or by means of adding the light only on a toned ground. In sketching in black and white, it is a good plan to accustom oneself to complete as one goes along, as far as may be, putting in outline and shadow together; but this needs a power of direct drawing and a correctness of eye only to be gained by continual practice. A slight preliminary basis of light lines to indicate the position and proportions, and yet not strong enough to need rubbing out, is also a good method for those who do not feel certain enough for the absolutely direct method of drawing.

Now in drawing, as I think I have pointed out before, no less than in all art, there are two main governing principles of working which may be distinguished.

I. The graphic aim.

II. The ornamental or decorative aim.

[206]

[207]

The Graphic Aim

[208]The graphic aim—the endeavour to represent a form exactly as it appears—a power always valuable to acquire whatever may be our ultimate purpose, leaves the draughtsman great freedom in the choice and use of line, or other means of obtaining relief, local tint, and tone.

In line-work the broad relief of the flat tones of shadow may be expressed in lines approaching the straight, diagonally sloping from right to left, or from left to right, as seems most natural to the action of the hand.

The quality of our lines will depend upon the quality we are seeking to express. We shall be led to vary them in seeking to express other characteristics, such as textures and surfaces.

In drawing fur or feathers, for instance, we should naturally vary the quality and direction of line, using broken lines and dots for the former, and flowing smooth fine lines for the latter, while extra force and relief would be gained by throwing them up upon solid black grounds. Solid black, also, to represent local colour, or material such as velvet, is often valuable as a contrast in black and white line-drawing, giving a richness of effect not to be obtained in any other way (see No. 2, p. 213). Its value was appreciated by the early German and Italian book-illustrators, and in our own time has been used almost to excess by some of our younger designers, who have been largely influenced by Hokusai and other Japanese artists, who are always skilful in the use of solid blacks.

In line-drawing a very useful principle to observe, to give solidity to figures and objects, is to let one's lines—say of drapery or shadow—run into solid blacks in the deepest interstices of the forms, as when folds of drapery are wrapped about a figure, or in the deeper folds themselves (No. 1, p. 213).

[209]

[210]The Ornamental Aim

I have spoken of the graphic and the ornamental aims as distinct, and so they may for practical purposes be regarded; although in some cases it is possible to combine a considerable amount of graphic force with decorative effect, and even in purely graphic art there should always be the controlling influence of the sense of composition which must be felt throughout all forms of art.

For the simplest ornamental function, however, very little graphic drawing is needed, over and above the very essential power of definition by pure outline, and feeling for silhouette; but a sense for the relief of masses upon a ground or field, and of the proportions and relations of lines and masses or distribution of quantities, is essential. Now an ornamental effect may be produced by the simple repetition of some form defined in outline arranged so as to fall into a rhythmic series of lines.

A series of birds upon a plan of this kind, for instance, would form a frieze on simple bordering in abstract line alone, and might be quite sufficient for some purposes. The same thing would be capable of more elaborate treatment and different effect by relieving the birds upon a darker ground, by defining the details of their forms more, or by alternating them in black or white, or by adopting the simple principle of counterchange (see p. 215).

[211]

Flowers or figures would be capable of the same simple and abstract treatment; and almost any form in nature, reduced to its simplest elements of recurring line and mass, and rhythmically [212]disposed, would give us distinct decorative motives.

The Ornamental Aim

It is quite open to the designer to select his lines and forms straight from nature, and, bearing in mind the necessity for selection of the best ornamental elements, for a certain simplification, and the rhythmical treatment before mentioned, it is good to do so, as the work is more likely to have a certain freshness than if some of the well-known historic forms of ornament are used again. We may, however, learn much from the ornamental use of these forms, and use similar forms as the boundaries of the shape of our pattern units and masses.

It is good practice to take a typical shape such as the Persian radiating flower or pine-apple, and use it as the plan for quite a different structure in detail, taking some familiar English flower as our motive. The same with the Indian and Persian palmette type. It is also desirable, as before pointed out, to draw sprays within formal boundaries for ornamental use. By such methods we may not only learn to appreciate the ornamental value of such forms, but by such adaptation and re-combination produce new varieties of ornament (see p. 217).

We may perceive how distinct are the two aims as between simple graphic drawing, or delineation, and what we call design, or conscious arrangements of line or form. While planes of relief, varied form and surface, values of light and shade, and accidental characteristics are rather the object with the graphic draughtsman, typical form and structure, and recurring line and mass, are [213]sought for by the ornamentist. Both series of facts, or qualities, or characteristics, are in nature.

Selection

[214]Judicious selection, however, is the test of artistic treatment; selection, that is, with a view to the aim and scope of the work. The truth of superficial appearance or accidental aspect is *one* sort of truth: the truth of the actual constructive characteristics—be they of figure, flower, or landscape—is *another.* Both belong to the thing we see—to the object we are drawing; but we shall dwell upon one truth or set of truths rather than the other, in accordance with our particular artistic aim, though, whatever this may be, and in whatever direction it may lead us, we shall find that selection of some sort will be necessary.

In making studies, however pure and simple, the object of which is to discover facts and to learn mastery of form, our aim should be to get as much truth as we can, truth of structure as well as of aspect. But these (as far as we can make them) exhaustive studies should be accompanied or followed by analytical studies made from different points of view and for different purposes.

Studies, for instance, made with a view to arrangements of *line* only—to get the characteristic and beautiful lines of a figure, a momentary attitude, the lines of a flower, or a landscape: studies with a view, solely, to the understanding of structure and form, or again, with the object of seizing the broad relations of light and shade, or tone and colour—all are necessary to a complete artistic education of the eye.

[215]

Accidents and Essentials

If we are drawn as students rather towards the picturesque and graphic side of art, we shall probably [216]look for accidents of line and form móre than what I should call the essentials, or *typical* line and form, which are the most valuable to the decorative designer.

In both directions some compact or compromise with nature is necessary in any really artistic re-presentation.

The painter and the sculptor often seek as *complete representation* as possible, and what may be called complete representation is within the range of their resources. Yet unless some individual choice or feeling impresses the work of either kind it is not a *re-presentation,* but becomes an *imitation,* and therefore inartistic.

The decorative designer and ornamentist seek to *suggest* rather than to *re-present,* though the decorator's suggestion of natural form, taking only enough to suit or express the particular ornamental purpose, must be considered also as a re-presentation. How much, or how little, he will take of actual nature must depend largely upon his resources, his object, and the limitations of his material—the conditions of his work in short; but his range may be as wide as from the flat silhouetted forms of stencils or simple inlays to the highly-wrought mural painting.

Design motive, individual conception and sentiment, apart from material, must, of course, always affect the question of the choice and degree of representation of nature. The painter will sometimes feel that he only wants to suggest forms, such as figures or buildings, half veiled in light and atmosphere, colours and forms in twilight, or half lost in luminous depths of shadow.

[217]

[218]

[219]

The Outward Vision and Inner Vision[220]

The decorative designer will sometimes want to emphasize forms with the utmost force and realism at his command, as in some crisp bit of carving or emphatic pattern, to give point and relief in his scheme of quantities.

There is no hard-and-fast rule in art, only general principles, constantly varied in practice, from which all principles spring, and into which, if vital, they ought to be capable of being again resolved.

But a design once started upon some principle—some particular motive of line or form—then, in following this out, it will seem to develop almost a life or law of growth of its own, which as a matter of logical necessity will demand a particular treatment—a certain natural consistency or harmony—from its main features down to the smallest detail as a necessity of its existence.

We might further differentiate art as, on the one hand, the image of the*outward vision*, and, on the other, as the outcome or image of the *inner vision.*

The first kind would include all portraiture, by which I mean faithful portrayal or transcript whether of animate or inanimate nature; while the second would include all imaginative conceptions, decorative designs, and pattern inventions.

The outward vision obviously relies upon what the eye perceives in nature. Its virtue consists in the faithfulness and truth of its graphic record, in the penetrating force of observation of fact, and the representative power by which they are reproduced on paper or canvas, clay or marble.

[221]

The image of the inner vision is also a record, but of a different order of fact. It may be often [222]of unconscious impressions and memories which are retained and recur with all or more than the vividness of actuality—the tangible forms of external nature calling up answering, but not identical, images in the mind, like reflections in a mirror or in still water, which are similar but never the same as the objects they reflect.

But the inner vision is not bound by the appearances of the particular moment. It is the record of the sum of many moments, and retains the typical impress of multitudinous and successive impressions—like the composite photograph, where faces may be printed one over another until the result is a more typical image than any individual one taken separately.

The inner vision sees the results of time rather than the impressions of the moment. It sees *space* rather than landscape: race rather than men: spirits rather than mortals: types rather than individuals.

The inner vision hangs the mind's house with a mysterious tapestry of figurative thoughts, a rich and fantastic imagery, a world where the elements are personified, where every tree has its dryad, and where the wings of the winds actually brush the cheek.

The inner vision re-creates rather than represents, and its virtue consists in the vividness and beauty with which, in the language of line, form, and colour, these visions of the mind are recorded and presented to the outward eye.

There is often fusion here again between two different tendencies, habits of mind, or ways of regarding things. In all art the mind must work [223]through the eye, whether its force appears in closeness of observation or in vivid imaginings. The very vividness of realization even of the most faithful portraiture is a testimony to mental powers.

The difference lies really in the *focus* of the mental force; and, in any case, the language of line and form we use will neither be forcible or convincing, neither faithful to natural fact nor true to the imagination, without close and constant study of external form and of its structure as well as its aspect.

[224]

CHAPTER IX

Of the Adaptation of Line and Form in Design, in various materials and methods—Mural Decoration—Fresco-work of the Italian Painters—Modern Mural Work—Mural Spacing and pattern Plans—Scale—The Skirting—The Dado—Field of the Wall—The Frieze—Panelling—Tapestry—Textile Design—Persian Carpets—Effect of Texture on Colour—Prints—Wall-paper—Stained Glass.

WE have been considering hitherto the choice and use of line and form, and various methods of their representation in drawing, both from the point of view of the graphic draughtsman and that of the ornamental designer.

We now come to consider the subject solely from the latter standpoint (the point of view of ornamental design); and it will be useful to endeavour to trace the principles governing the selection of form and use of line as influenced by some of the different methods and conditions of craftsmanship, and as adapted to various decorative purposes.

Mural Decoration

The most important branch of decorative art may be said to be mural decoration, allied as it is with the fundamental constructive art of all—architecture, from which it obtains its determining conditions and natural limitations.

Its history in the past is one of splendour and dignity, and its record includes some of the finest [225]art ever produced. The ancient Asiatic nations were well aware of its value not only as decoration but as a record.

The palace and temple and tomb-walls of ancient Egypt, Persia, and Assyria vividly illustrate the life and ideas of those peoples, while they conform to mural conditions. The painted council halls and churches of the Middle Ages fulfil the same purpose in a different spirit; but mural decoration in its richest, most imaginative and complete form was developed in Italy, from the time of Giotto, whose famous works at the Arena Chapel at Padua and Assisi are well known, to the time of Michael Angelo, who in the sublime ceiling of the Sistine Chapel seemed to touch the extreme limits of mural work, and in fact might be said to have [226]almost *defied* them, painting mouldings in relief and in perspective to form the framework of pictures where figures on different scales are used. In the Sistine Chapel the series of earlier frescoes on the lower wall by Botticelli, Lorenzo di Credi, Ghirlandajo, Pinturicchio, and other Florentine painters of the fifteenth century are really more strictly mural in feeling, and safer as guides in general treatment, than the work of the great master himself. They have much of the repose and richness as well as the quiet decorative effect of tapestry.

Fresco-Work of Italian Painters

The frescoes in the Palazzo Publico at Siena, Pinturicchio's work in the Piccolomini Chapel and the Appartimenti Borgia, the Campo Santo at Pisa and the Riccardi Chapel of Benozzo Gozzoli at Florence, may be mentioned as among the gems of mural painting.

Modern Mural Work

We have but little important mural painting in this country. Doubtless, from various traces discovered under Puritan whitewash, the walls of our mediæval churches were painted as frequently as in continental countries, but so completely did artistic tradition and religious sentiment change after the Reformation that the opportunities have been few and the encouragement less for mural painting. An attempt to revive fresco-painting was made in our Houses of Parliament, and various scenes from our national history have been rendered with varying degrees of merit; but they have chiefly demonstrated the need of continuous practice in such work on the part of our painters and the absence of a true decorative instinct.

It is to the honour of Manchester that her [227]Town Hall contains one of the most important and interesting pieces of mural painting by one of the most original of modern English artists—Ford Madox Brown—a work conceived in the true spirit of mural work, being a record of local [228]history, as well as a decoration, while distinctly modern in sentiment and showing strong dramatic feeling, as well as historical knowledge.

The chapel on which Mr. F. J. Shields is engaged in London will probably be unique in its way as a complete piece of mural decoration by an English artist of singular individuality, sincerity, and power, as well as decorative ability.

But unfortunately opportunities for important mural decoration of this kind are very rare in England. The art is not popularized: we have no school of trained mural designers, and we have no public really interested. Our commercial system and system of house tenure are against it. Our only chance is in public buildings, which indeed have always been its best field. Yet we neglect, I think, a most important educational influence. The painted churches and public halls of the Middle Ages filled in a great measure the place of public libraries. A painted history, a portrait, a dramatic or romantic incident told in the vivid language of line, form, and colour, is stamped upon the memory never to be forgotten. It would be possible, I think, to impart a tolerably exact knowledge of the sequence of history, of the conditions of life at different epochs, of great men and their work, from a well-imagined series of mural paintings, without the aid of books; and in this direction, perhaps, our school walls would present an appropriate field.

Modern opportunities of mural decoration are chiefly domestic. The country mansion, or the modest home of the suburban citizen, affords the principal field in our time for the exercise of the [229]taste or ingenuity of the wall-decorator. In this comparatively restricted field, taste is perhaps of more consequence than any other quality. A sense of appropriateness, a harmonizing faculty, a power of arrangement of simple materials—these are invaluable, for, more than any others, they go to the making of a livable interior.

Mural Spacing and Pattern Plans

On first thought it would almost seem as if the designer was less technically restricted in this direction of mural work than any other; yet he will soon feel that he cannot produce an artistic and thoughtful scheme without taking many things into consideration which really belong to the conditions or natural limitations of his work.

There is, firstly, the idea of the wall itself—part of the house-structure—a shelter and protection or boundary. It is no part of a designer's business to put anything upon the wall in the way of decoration which will induce anyone to forget that it is a wall—nothing to disturb the flatness and repose.

The four walls of a room inclose a space to dwell in, in comfort and security. The windows show us outward real life and nature. The walls should not compete with the windows. Nature must be translated into the terms of line and form and colour, and invention and fancy may be pleasantly suggestive in the harmonious metre and rhythm of pattern.

A wall surface extends horizontally and vertically, but the vertical extension seems to assert itself most to the eye.

Any arrangement of lines of the trellis or diaper order logically covers a wall surface, and may be appropriately used as a basis for a wall pattern, [230]whether merely to mark the positions of a simple spray or formal sprig pattern, or as a ground-plan for a completely filled field of repeating ornament, whether painted, stencilled, or in the form of wall-paper or textile hanging.

In the simple geometric net of squares or diamonds or circles, however, there is nothing that emphatically marks adaptability to a vertical position. Such plans in themselves are equally appropriate to the floor in the form of paving and parquet. The ogee plan, however, and its variant, the vertical serpentine or spiral plan, at once suggest vertical extension, the former perhaps by its leaf-like points arranging themselves scale-wise, and the latter by its suggestion of ascending movement.

It is noteworthy that in the course of the historic evolution of mural decoration, designs based upon these systems constantly recur. They are part of the pattern-designer's vocabulary of line, and among the principal, though simplest, terms by which he is able to express vertical extension.

The question of *scale* in designing mural decoration of any sort is very important. This demands a certain power of realizing the effect of certain lines and masses if carried out, and the relation of one part to another as well as to the dimensions of the walls and the room itself. Here, as indeed throughout art, a reference to the human figure will give us our key, since after all decoration goes to form a background for humanity. With natural flowers and leaves it is always right to design for mural purposes on the same scale as nature.

[231]

Scale

Scale in design should be also considered in [232]relation to the general character of a building and its purpose, the use and lighting of a living room: its dimensions and proportions, and relation to other rooms. There is great range for individual taste and fancy.

The artist would naturally look to the capacity of the space which he had to decorate, and what it suggested to his mind. He might want to emphasize a long, low room by horizontal lines, or to accentuate a lofty one by verticals.

By the judicious use of line and scale in design, the designer holds a certain power of transformation in his hands, not to speak of the transforming effect of colour of different keys and tones, the apparent contraction or expansion of surfaces by patterns of different character and scale.

It would obviously not do to regard any wall merely as so much expanse of surface available for sketching unrelated groups and figures upon, as they might be jotted down in a sketch-book, and to offer it as decoration. In an interior thus treated, we should lose all sense of repose, dignity, and proportion.

Use and custom, which fix and determine so many things in social life without written laws, have also prescribed certain divisions of the wall, which, in regard to the exigencies of life and habit and modern conditions generally, seem natural enough.

[233]

The Skirting

The lower parts of the walls of most modern dwellings being generally occupied by furniture placed against them, and liable to be soiled or injured, it would be out of place to put important and elaborate ornament or figure designs extending [234]to the skirting. The wooden skirting, of about nine inches or a foot in depth, which is placed along the foot of the wall in our modern rooms, is the armour-plating to protect the plaster, which otherwise might be chipped and litter the floor. It is perhaps the last relic of the more substantial and extensive wood panelling and wainscotting which, up to the latter part of the last century, covered the lower walls of the more comfortable houses, and has been revived in our own day. The decorator may use panelling, or wainscotting, or a simple chair-rail above plain painting, wall-paper, dado, or stencilling, or a dado of matting, as methods of covering, and at the same time decorating, the lower walls of rooms.

The use of the dado of a darker colour and of wainscot is, no doubt, due to considerations of wear and tear, and so, like the origin of much ornamental art, may be traced to actual use and constructive necessity. When the wood-work of a room—the doors and window frames—is of the same colour and character as the dado, a certain agreeable unity is preserved, and it forms a useful plain framing to set off the patterned parts of the wall. This wainscot or dado framing with the wood-work should be as to colour arranged to suit the general scheme adopted. Where paint is used, white for the wood-work usually has the best effect.

[235]

Field of the Wall

The largest space of wall occurs above the chair-rail, or dado, and, according to modern habits and usage, portable property in the shape of framed pictures, etc., is usually placed here [236]along the eye-line, so that any decoration on this—the main field of the wall—is regarded as subsidiary to what is placed upon it; but, of course, pictures can be used as the central points of a decorative scheme. On the upper part of a wall, below the plaster cornice, the mural designer has the chance of putting a frieze, and a frieze usually gives the effect of additional height to a room, besides enriching the wall.

An effective treatment of a large room, and one which is more reposeful than cutting up the wall into these portions, as in dado, field, and frieze, is to carry up wood panelling to the frieze, and let this (the frieze) be the important decorative feature.

Supposing the room was twelve feet high, one could afford to have eight feet of panelling, and then a frieze of four feet deep. In this case one would look for an interesting painted frieze of figures—some legend or story to run along the four sides of the room, and in such a case it might be marked with considerable pictorial freedom.

More formal figure design or ornamental work in coloured plaster-work, stucco, and gesso could also be appropriately used in such a position, as also on the ceiling.

Now as regards choice of line and form in their relation to the decoration of such mural spaces. Taking the lower wall, dado, or panelling, one reason why panelling has so agreeable an effect is, I think, that the series of vertical and horizontal lines seem to express the proportions, while they emphasize the flatness and repose of the wall, and when used beneath a painted frieze they lead the eye upwards, forming a quiet framing of rectangular [237]lines below to the ornate and varied design of the frieze. Where we are limited to decorating a wall by means of plain painting, stencils, or wall-paper, this idea of reposeful constructive lines and forms on the lower wall should still dominate upon the field. Subject to our repeating plan we may be freer both in line and form, using free scrolls, branch-work, fruit, and flower masses at pleasure, because the space is more extended, and we shall feel the necessity in a repeating pattern of spreading adequately over it; but such designs, however fine in detail, should be constructed upon a more or less geometric base or plan. We are, as regards the main field of the wall, still unavoidably, though not disadvantageously, influenced by the tradition of the textile hanging or arras tapestry, no doubt; and certainly there is no more rich and comfortable lining for living rooms than tapestry, or, at the same time, more reposeful and decoratively satisfying. But, of course, where we can afford arras tapestry (such as the superb work of William Morris and his weavers), we ought not to allow anything to compete with it upon the same wall. It is sufficient in itself.

Tapestry

Of what splendour of colour and wealth of decorative and symbolical invention tapestry was capable in the past may be seen in magnificent Burgundian specimens of the fifteenth century, now in the South Kensington Museum.

Tapestry hangings of a repeating pattern and quiet colour could be used appropriately beneath painted upper walls, or a frieze, as no doubt frequently was the custom in great houses in the Middle Ages.

Appartimenti Borgia[238]

In the Appartimenti Borgia in the Vatican, for instance, which consists of lofty vaulted rooms with frescoes by Pinturicchio upon the upper walls between the spans of the vaulting, and upon the vaulting itself, we may see, about eleven feet from the floor, along the moulding, the hooks left for the tapestry hangings, which completed the decoration of the room. The lower walls are now largely occupied by book-shelves; but books themselves may form a pleasant background, as one may often observe in libraries, especially when the bindings are rich and good in tone: and here, too, we get our verticals and horizontals again.

So long as the feeling for the repose and flatness of the wall surface is preserved, there are no special limitations in the choice of form. It becomes far more a matter of *treatment of form and subject* in perfectly appropriate mural design. There is one principle, however, which seems to hold good in the treatment of important figure subjects to occupy the main wall surfaces as panels: while pictorial realization of a kind may be carried quite far, it is desirable to avoid large masses of light sky, or to attempt much in the way of atmospheric effect. It is well to keep the horizon high, and, if sky is shown, to break it with architecture and trees.

Still more important is it to observe this in tapestry. It is very noticeable how tapestry design declined after the fifteenth century or early years of the sixteenth, when perspective and pictorial planes were introduced, and sky effects to emulate painting, and thus the peculiarly mural feeling was lost, with its peculiar beauty, richness, and repose.

[239]

[240]In the translation into tapestry even of so tapestry-like a picture as that of Botticelli's "Primavera," it is noteworthy how Mr. Morris has felt the necessity of reducing the different planes, and the chiaroscuro of the painting, by more leafy and floral detail; making it, in short, more of a pattern than a picture.

The Frieze

A frieze is susceptible of a much more open, lighter, and freer treatment than a field. A frieze is one of the mural decorator's principal means of giving lightness and relief to his wall. In purely floral and ornamental design the field of close pattern, formal diaper, or sprigs at regular intervals may be appropriately relieved by bolder lines and masses, and a more open treatment in the frieze. The frieze, too, affords a means of contrast in line to the line system of the field of the wall, its horizontal expression usefully opposing the verticals or diagonals of the wall pattern below. The frieze may be regarded as a horizontal border, and in border designs the principle of transposition of the relation of pattern to ground is a useful one to bear in mind, as leading always to an effective result. I mean, supposing our field shows a pattern mainly of light upon dark, the frieze might be on the reverse plan, a dark pattern on a light ground.

And whereas, as I have said, one would exclude wide light spaces from our mural field, in the frieze one might effectively show a light sky ground throughout, and arrange a figure or floral design upon that.

The principle governing the treatment of main and lower wall spaces or fields, which teaches the designer to preserve the repose of the surface, may [241]be said to rule also in all textile design, and textile design has, as we have seen in the form of tapestry, and hangings of all kinds, a very close association with mural decoration.

Textile Design

Any textile may be considered, from the designer's point of view, as presenting so much *surface* [242]for pattern, whether that surface is hung upon a wall, or curtains a door or a window, or is spread in the form of carpets or rugs upon floors, or over the cushions of furniture, or adapts itself to the variety of curve surface and movement of the human form in dress materials and costume. Textile beauty is beauty of material and surface, and unless the pattern or design upon it or woven with it enhances that beauty of material and surface, and becomes a part of the expression of that material and surface, it is better without pattern.

To place informal shaded flowers and leaves upon a carpet, for instance, where the warp is very emphatic, and the process of weaving necessitates a stepped or rectangularly broken outline, is to mistake appropriate decorative effect, capacity of material, and position in regard to the eye. We cannot get away, in a carpet, from the idea of a flat field starred with more or less formal flowers, and colour arrangements which owe their richness and beauty, not to the relief of shading, but to the heraldic principle of relieving one tint or colour upon another. The rich inlay of colour which a Persian or any Eastern carpet presents is owing to its being designed upon this principle; and in Persian work that peculiarly rich effect of colour, apart from fine material, is owing to the principle of the use of outlines of different colours defining and relieving the different forms in the pattern upon different grounds. The rectangular influence arising from the technical conditions of the work gives a definite textile character to the design [243]which is very agreeable; besides, as a question of line and form, in a carpet or rug which is rectangular [244]in shape and laid usually upon rectangular floors, the squareness of form harmonizes with the conditions and surroundings of the work in use. The Persian designer, indeed, appears to be so impressed with this feeling, that he uses a succession of borders around the central field of his carpet or rug, still further emphasizing the rectangularity; while he avoids the too rigid effect of a series of straight lines which the crossing of the threads of the weft at right angles to the warp might cause, by changing the widths of his subsidiary borders and breaking them with a constant variety of small patterns, and inserting narrow white lines between the black lines of the border.

Effect of Texture on Colour

In tapestry the effect of the emphatic warp worked vertically in the loom, but hung horizontally, has a very important influence upon the effect. If we took a piece of paper coloured with a flat even tint, and folded it in ridges, the quality of the tint would be at once changed, and so in tapestry the passing of the wool of the wefts, which form the pattern or picture, over the strong lines of the warp—which are broad enough to take the outlines of the cartoon upon them—produces that soft and varied play of colour—really colour in light and shade—which, over and above the actual dyes and artistic selection of tints, gives the peculiar charm and effect in tapestry.

This sheen and variety are more or less evident in all textiles, and a good textile pattern only adds to the variety and richness of the surface. [245]The different thicknesses or planes of surface and the difference of their texture caused by the different wefts being brought to the surface of the [246]cloth or silk (from the simplest contrast of line presented by the simplest arrangements of warp and weft, to the complexities of many-coloured silk stuffs and brocade) alone give a value to the surface pattern.

In cut velvet the same principle of contrast of surface is emphasized still further, the rich deep nap of the less raised parts contrasting pleasantly with the mat effect of the ground.

In designs for such material one should aim at boldly blocked-out patterns in silhouette—bold leaf and fruit forms say—designed on the principle of the stencil.

Prints

With prints the range is of course freer, the material itself suggesting something lighter and more temporary. It seems highly probable that printed cotton was originally a substitute for embroidered linen or more sumptuous materials. There are certainly instances of very similar patterns in Indian and Persian work in silk embroidery, and also in printed cotton. In some cases the print is partly embroidered, which seems to mark a transitional stage, and recalls the lingering use of illumination in the early days of the printing press, in another department of art.

Anything that will repeat as a pattern in what can be produced by line, dot, and tints of colour, and engraved upon wood-blocks or copper rollers, can be printed of course; and, as is generally the case with an art which has no very obvious technical [247]limitations, it is liable to be caught by the imitative spirit, and cheap and rapid production and demand for novelties (so-called) generally end [248]in loss of taste and deterioration of quality, especially in design. From the artistic point of view we can only correct this by bearing in mind similar considerations to those which hold good as general principles and guides in designing for textiles generally, having regard to the object, purpose, and position—to the ultimate use of the material, and differentiating our designs, as in the case of other textile design accordingly.

Thus in the matter of plan and direction of line and character of form we shall at once find natural distinctions and divisions, as our design is for hanging, or spreading horizontally, or wearing; and these different functions will also determine scale and choice and treatment of form and colour.

There is no doubt that with patterns printed more range may be allowed than with patterns to be woven, where line and form are both controlled by the necessities of being reproduced by so many points to the inch. At the same time the object of all design and pattern work being the greatest beauty compatible with the material and conditions, one should seek, not such effects as merely test the capacity or ingenuity of the machine, but rather such as appear to be most decoratively appropriate and effective.

There appears to be no *mechanical* reason why cotton should not be printed all over with landscapes and graphic sketches, and people clothe themselves with them as with Christmas numbers, or turn their couches, chairs, and curtains into scrap albums, but there is every reason *on the score of taste* why these things should not be done.

[249]

[250]With any textile, as I have said, we are as designers dealing with surface. It is surface ornament that is wanted also in printed cotton. Now good line and form and pure tints have the best effect, because they do not break the surface into holes, and give a ragged or tumbled appearance, which accidental bunches of darkly-shaded flowers in high relief undoubtedly do. If small rich detail and variety are wanted, we should seek it in the inventive spirit of the Persian and Indian, and break our solid colours with mordants or arabesques in colour of delicate subsidiary pattern instead of using coarse planes of light and shadow, or showing up ragged and unrelated forms upon violent grounds.

[251]

The true idea of a print pattern is of something gay and fanciful: bright and fresh in colour, and clear in line and form: a certain quaintness is allowable, and in purely floral designs there is room for a considerable degree of what might be called naturalism, so far as good line-drawing and understanding of flower form goes, emphasis of colour being sought by means of *planes of colour*, rather than by planes of shadow.

I had intended to touch upon other provinces of design, but I have taken up so much space with those I have been discussing already that I can only now briefly allude to these.

Wall-Paper

Of wall-paper, which may be regarded in the light of more or less of a substitute for mural painting, and also textile wall-hangings, much the same general principles and many of the same remarks apply as have been already used in regard to mural decoration. The designer has [252]much freedom as to motive, and his ingenuity is only bounded by or concentrated in a square of twenty-one inches. If he has succeeded in making an agreeable pattern which will repeat not too obviously over an indefinite space, to form a not obtrusive background, and which can be printed and sold to the ordinary citizen, he is supposed to have satisfied the conditions.

But he may be induced to go further and attempt the design of a complete decoration as far as dado, field, frieze, and ceiling go; and this would involve all the thought necessary to the mural painter, narrowed down to the exigencies of mechanical repeat.

Allied to the wall is the window, and in glazing and the art of the glass-painter we have another very distinct and beautiful sphere of line design. In plain leading the same law of covering vertical surface holds good as to selection of plan and system of line: almost any simple geometric net is appropriate, if not too complex or small in form to hold glass or to permit lead to follow its lines. Leaded panels of roundels (or "bull's eyes") of plain glass have a good effect in casements where a sparkle of light rather than outward view is sought for.

Stained Glass

When we come to designing for stained glass we should still bear in mind the fundamental net of lead lines which forms the basis of our pattern, or glass picture, as it were: and the designer's object should be to make it good as an arrangement of line independently of the colour, while practical to the glazier.

[253]

Although lead is very pliable, too much must [254]not be expected of it in the way of small depressions and angles: the boundary lines of the figures, which should be the boldest of all, should be kept as simple as possible, not only on this account, but because complex outlines cannot well be cut in glass. A head, for instance, is inclosed in sweeping line, and the profile defined within the lead line by means of painting. A hand would be defined on the same principle. Each different colour demands a different inclosure of lead, although in the choice of glass much variation of tint can be obtained, as in the case of pot metal running from thin to thick glass, which intensifies the colour, and many kinds of what is called flashed. Yet to the designer, from the point of view of line, glass design is a kind of translucent mosaic, in which the primal technical necessity of the leading which holds the glory of the coloured light together, really enhances its splendour, and in affording opportunities for decoration and expressive linear composition imparts to the whole work its particular character and beauty.

This after all is the principle to cling to in all designing, to adapt our designs to the particular distinctive character and beauty of the material for which they are destined, to endeavour to think them out in those materials, and not only on paper. Whatever the work may be—carving, inlays, modelling, mosaic, textiles—through the whole range of surface decoration, we should think out our designs, not only in relation to the limitations of their material, but also in their relation to each other, to their effect in actual use, and even to their possible use in association [255]together, which, of course, is of paramount importance in designing a complete room or any comprehensive piece of decoration.

And when we leave plane surfaces and seek to invent appropriate, that is to say, *expressive* ornament allied to concave and convex surfaces, to the varied forms of pottery for instance, metal-work, and glass vessels, furniture, and accessories of all kinds, we shall find the same laws and principles hold good which should guide us in all design—to adapt design to the characteristics and conditions of the material, to its structural capacity, its use and purpose, as well as to use or invention in line, both as a controlling plan or base of ornament, as well as a means of the association and expression of form.

[256]

CHAPTER X

Of the Expression and Relief of Line and Form by *Colour*—Effect of same Colour upon different Grounds—Radiation of Colour—White Outline to clear Colours—Quality of Tints relieved upon other Tints—Complementaries—Harmony—The Colour Sense—Colour Proportions—Importance of Pure Tints—Tones and Planes—The Tone of Time—Pattern and Picture—A Pattern not necessarily a Picture, but a Picture in principle a Pattern—Chiaroscuro—Examples of Pattern-work and Picture-work—Picture-patterns and Pattern-pictures.

PERHAPS the most striking means of the expression of relief of line and form, certainly the most attractive, is by colour. By colour we obtain the most complete and beautiful means of expression in art.

Relief of Line and Form by Colour

Our earliest ideas of form are probably derived through the different colours of objects around us, by which they are thrown into relief upon the background, or against other objects; and, as I mentioned in the first chapter, we reach outline by observing the edges of different masses relieved as dark or light upon light or dark grounds, so now, in my last, we come again to the consideration of the definition of line and form by colour, and their relief and expression upon different planes or fields of colour.

[257]

There is first the colour of the object itself—the local colour—and then the colour of the ground [258]upon which it is relieved, both of which in their action and reaction upon each other will greatly affect the value of the local colour and the degree of relief of the form upon it.

One of the best and simplest ways to ascertain the real value of a colour and its effect upon different grounds or fields is to take a flower—say a red poppy, and place it against a white paper ground, blocking in the local colour as relieved upon white, as near as may be to its full strength, with a brush, and defining the form as we go along. Then try the same flower upon grounds of different tints—green, blue, yellow—and it will be at once perceived what a different value and expression the same form in the same colour has upon different tinted grounds. A scarlet poppy would appear clearest and darkest upon white; it would show a tendency upon a blue ground to blend or blur at its edges, and also on yellow and green to a less extent.

It is this tendency to lose the edges of forms owing to the radiation of colours, and to mingle with the colour of the background, which makes a strong outline so constantly a necessity in decorative work. One may use a black on a white, a brown, or a gold outline (as in cloisonné), the nature of the outline being generally determined by the nature of the work. In stained glass the outline must be black, and this black is of the greatest value in enhancing by opposition the brilliance of the colours of the glass it incloses, stopping out the light around it as it does in solid lead when placed in the window.

[259]

Clearing Coloured Forms

A white outline produced by a resist or a mordant [260]in a printed textile, where the colours used are full and rich, often has a good effect, lightening the effect while giving point and definition to certain leading forms. Instances of the use of white outlines may be found in Eastern carpets, where the main colours, being dark blue and yellows on rich red, are relieved in parts by a dull white outline. Also in Persian carpets of the sixteenth or seventeenth century, the scrollwork in red is often relieved by an ivory white outline on blue.

It is always a good practice in blocking in flowers, either from nature or as parts of a design, to leave a white outline at the junctions—that is to say, where one petal overlaps another, or where there is a joint in the stem, or a fold in the leaf—and to show the ribbings, markings, and divisions of flower and leaf.

By judiciously changing the quality of our tints it is possible to make different colours in a pattern tell clearly. To relieve red upon blue, for instance, one would use an orange red upon greenish blue, or scarlet upon a gray blue—the general principle being apparently a kind of compensating balance between colours, so that in taking from one you give to another.

A full red and blue used together, as we have seen, would show a tendency to purple, unless separated by outlines; so that if the blue was full and rich, the red would have to approach brown or russet; or if the red was a full one—a crimson red—the blue would have to approach green.

Harmony

This may be because of the necessary complements in colours, which we see in nature, and [261]which prepossess the eye, and make it demand these modifications to satisfy the sense of harmony.

When daylight struggles with candle- or lamp-light, one may notice that upon the white cloth of a dinner-table the light is blue and the shadows yellow or orange—the orange deepening as with the fading daylight the blue grows deeper, until the colour of the light and the shadow change places. The same principle may be noticed in firelight, but the redder the flame the greener will be the shadows.

Harmony in colour may be said to consist—apart from the general acknowledgment of the law of complementaries, in giving quality to the raw pigments by gradation, by a certain admixture or infusion of other colours.

To begin with the negatives—white and black—white may be creamy or silvery; black may be of a greenish or a bluish or brownish tone; then the primaries—red, blue, yellow, or red, green, violet—red may range from crimson to orange and russet; yellow may approach green or gold; green may be first cousin to blue; blue may be turquoise on the one hand, and touch purple upon the other; and so on through infinite variations of half tints and tones.

No doubt it is an easier matter to harmonize half tints than full bright colours, which may account for the prevalence of the former in decorative work. Nature's pattern-book, too, is full of half tones and mixed tints.

The Colour Sense

We may not all see colour precisely in the same way, and the same colour may appear to be of a different tint to different eyes; and it seems [262]certain that climate and surroundings affect the colour sense: light and colour will stimulate the delight in colour; while, where grayness and dullness characterize the surroundings of life, the colour sense will grow weak, or, if it is manifested at all, it will show a tendency to grayness and heaviness of tint.

The art of the different peoples of the world illustrates this, and, as we may see by turning from east to west, or from north to south, or even from winter to summer, in the main the love of colour follows the sun, like the rainbow.

We can all do something to cultivate our sense of colour, however, and there is no better way than studying the harmonies and varieties of nature. Even the town-dweller is not altogether deprived of the sight of the sky, which constantly unfolds the most beautiful compositions both of form and colour.

As to the choice of colours in decorative design, so far as that is not narrowed by the particular conditions of the work, we must be guided by much the same considerations as would serve us in designing generally, and must, of course, think of appropriateness to position and purpose. Much depends, too, upon proportions of colour, and a beautiful and harmonious effect may be produced in a room by keeping the colour in a particular key, or even delicately varying the designs and tints of one or two colours. The same might be said in arranging a scheme of colouring for any particular piece of design—say, a painted panel or a textile pattern; although such things must ultimately be governed by their relation to other [263]parts in any general scheme—circumstances necessitate their being often designed apart. Still, if the colour of a pattern has been carefully thought out, or rather harmoniously felt, as a real organic thing, it is sure to fit into its place when its time comes.

In arranging our design of colour we can have no better guide, as to proportions and quality, than nature, and should do well, as a matter of practice, to take a flower, or the plumage of a bird, or the colours of a landscape, and adapt them to some particular pattern or scheme of decoration, following the relative degrees of tint and their quantities as nearly as possible. To do this successfully requires some invention and taste; but successful, or unsuccessful, one could hardly fail to learn something positive and valuable about colour, if the attempt was conscientiously made; and fresher motives and sweeter colour would be more likely to result from such study.

Importance of Pure Tints

I think it is a very important thing in all decorative work to keep one's colours pure in quality, and to avoid muddy or heavy tints. Brown is an especially difficult colour to use, because of its generally heavy effect as a pigment, and the difficulty of harmonizing it with other colours except as an outline; and even here it makes all the difference whether it is a cool or a hot shade. A hot brown is most destructive of harmony in colours. It is safe, as a rule, to make it lean to green, or bronze, or gold.

As a general rule it is well to work either in a range of cool tints—a cool key of colour, or the [264]reverse—a warm and rich one. Few cool harmonies can be better than ultramarine and turquoise on greenish white, of which the Persians and Indians are so fond in tile-work. They are delightful to the eye, while peculiarly adapted to the work, owing their quality to the oxide of copper, which the firing brings out so well.

Blues and greens and grays, relieved with white and yellow and orange: or, reds and yellows, relieved with white and opposed by blacks, generally answer: or a range of reds together, or range of blues, or of yellows, with black and white for contrast and accent. Blue and white, too, can be modified in quality; black may be greenish in tone, or brownish, bluish, or purplish according to the harmony aimed at. White may be pure or ivory-toned, cream-coloured or influenced by other colours, and should vary in degree according to the strength of the harmony. This brings us to the question of tone.

Tones and Planes

Now the ornamentist, the designer of patterns, relies for his effect upon the use of certain planes and oppositions of tints to relieve and express his design, to emphasize its main motive, to bring out or to subdue its lines and forms. He knows that cool flat tints—blues, greens, grays—will make forms and surfaces retire, and he makes use of them for flat and reposeful effects, such as wall and ceiling surfaces, adopting the natural principle of colour in landscape and sky.

He uses richer and more varied colour in textile hangings and carpets, furniture, and accessories—reds, yellows, greens, crimson, russets, orange, gold—which answer to the brighter flowers and [265]parterres of our gardens, as things to be near the eye and touch, and to occur as lesser quantities in a scheme of interior colour design.

In the colour design of patterns, harmonious and rich effects can be produced by the use of pure colour alone, no doubt, if carefully proportioned, and separated by outline; though harmony is more difficult to attain in pure colours used in their full strength; and for their due effect, and to avoid harshness, such a treatment really requires out-door light or special conditions of lighting, or the strong light of eastern or southern countries, to soften the effect.

And since we have to adapt our designs to their probable surroundings, we usually consciously select certain tones or shades of a colour, rather than use it absolutely pure or in its full strength. The beautiful tone which time gives to all colour-work is difficult to rival, but no conscious imitation of it is tolerable.

But so long as our aim is strictly to make a colour scheme of any kind in relation to itself, or in harmony with its conditions, we are on a safe and sound path. It is this relativity which is the important thing in all decorative art, and which, more distinctly than any other quality, distinguishes it from pictorial art; although pictorial art is under the necessity of the same law in regard to itself; and in its highest forms, as in mural work, is certainly subject to relativity in its widest sense.

Pattern and Picture

At first sight it might appear as if there were an essential fundamental natural difference between a pattern and a picture, but when we come [266]to consider it, it appears to be rather a distinction than a difference.

A pattern may be an arrangement of lines, forms, and a harmony of planes and tones of colour.

But these words would describe in general terms a picture also.

Certain recurrences of line and form; certain re-echoing notes of the same, or allied colour, are necessary to both pattern and picture. The abstract ingredients appear to be the same in both cases.

A picture indeed may be considered as a pattern of another sort, and the real difference is that whereas a pattern is not necessarily a picture, a picture is bound to be a pattern—a pattern having its quantities, its balance of masses, its connecting lines, its various planes, its key of colour, its play of contrasts, its harmony of tones.

Technically, a picture may be considered as an *informal* pattern, mainly of tone and values; while a pattern may be considered as a *formal* pattern, mainly of planes of colour.

The ancient art of the East was all frankly pattern-work, whatever the subject pictured. Egyptian, Persian, Indian, Chinese, Moorish and Arabian art, in all their varieties, show the dominating sense of pattern, and the invention of the instinctive decorators in the use of colour.

The Japanese, also, are instinctive decorators, though in a less formal and more impressionistic way, and with much more naturalistic feeling. Their pictures printed from colour blocks, as well as their "kakimonos," painted on silk, are frankly [267]pattern-pictures, the pattern motive being quite as strong or stronger than the graphic or representative motive.

Mediæval and early Renaissance painting in Europe was frankly more or less formal and of the nature of ornament, and even in its freest and fullest development, in the works of the great masters of the sixteenth century of Venice and Florence, a certain decorative or architectural feeling was never forgotten.

Painting was still in close association with architecture, and was the chief adornment of churches and palaces; thus it preserved a peculiar distinction and dignity of style. The Dutch school did more perhaps to break these old decorative and architectural traditions than any other, with their domestic and purely naturalistic motives, their pursuit of realism, atmospheric effect, and chiaroscuro—that fascinating goal of painting.

Chiaroscuro

Yet there were some of the seventeenth-century masters, and of the best, such as De Hooghe and Ver Meer of Delft, who showed themselves very much alive to decorative effect, which their power of chiaroscuro—the power of painting things in their proper atmosphere, as lost in transparent depths of shadow, or found in luminous mystery—only seemed to enhance.

As a wonderful instance of ornamental and dignified design carried into every detail with most careful draughtsmanship, and yet beautiful in chiaroscuro and grave colour, there is no finer [268]example than J. Van Eyck's portrait-picture of "Jan Arnolfini and his Wife" in our National Gallery. Such pictures as these would tell as [269]rich and precious gems upon the wall, and would form the centres to which the surrounding colour patterns and decoration would lead up, as in the picture the little mirror reflecting the figures shines upon the wall, a picture within a picture.

It is instructive from any point of view to study the quantities and relations of colour, and their tones and values, in such works.

Ver Meer of Delft[270]

Take Ver Meer's "Lady at a Spinet" in our National Gallery.

We have a plain white wall, exquisite in tone, upon which the crisp gold of the small picture inclosing a brownish landscape with a blue and white sky, and the broad black frame of the picture of Cupid tell strongly, yet fall into plane behind the figure in white satin—quite a different quality of white, and warmer and brighter than the wall. The bodice is a steely blue silk, which is repeated in the velvet seat of the chair; while the blue and white landscape upon the open lid of the spinet repeats the blue and white landscape on the wall, and the blue and white motive is subtly re-echoed in a subdued key in the little tiles lining the base of the wall. The floor is a chequer of black and white (mottled) marble, which gives a fine relief to the dress and repeats the emphatic black of the picture frame; the stand of the spinet is also black striated marble. Quiet daylight falls through the greenish white of the leaded panes. The pink-brown woodwork of the spinet and chair prevent the colour scheme from being cold. The flesh is very pale and ivory-like in tone, but the dress is enlivened by little crisp scarlet and gold touches in the narrow laces which tie the sleeves.

The little picture is a gem of painting and truth of tone, and at the same time might well suggest a charming scheme of colour to an ornamentist.

Van Eyck

Examine the Van Eyck in the same way, and we shall find a very rich but quiet scheme of colour in a lower key, highly decorative, yet presented with extraordinary realistic force, united with extreme refinement and exquisite chiaroscuro, and [271]truth of tone and value, as a portrait-picture, and piece of interior lighting.

It is like taking an actual peep into the inner life of a Flemish burgher of the fifteenth century.

One seems to breathe the still air of the quiet room, the gray daylight falling through the leaded casements, one of which stands open, and shows a narrow strip of luminous sky and suggestion of a garden with scarlet blossoms in green leaves.

The man is clad in a long mantle of claret-brown velvet edged with fur, over black tunic and hose. He wears a quaint black hat upon his head, which almost foreshadows the tall hat of the modern citizen. The pale strange face looks paler and stranger beneath it, but is in character with the long thin hands. The figure gives one the impression of legal precision and dryness, and a touch of clerical formality. The wife is of a buxom and characteristic Flemish type, in a grass-green robe edged with white fur, over peacock blue; a crisp silvery white head-dress; a dark red leather belt with silver stitching. Her figure is relieved upon the subdued red of the bed hangings, continued in the cover of the settle and the red clogs. The wall of the room, much lost in transparent shade, is of a greenish gray tone, and in the centre, between the figures, a circular convex mirror sparkles on the wall reflecting the backs of the figures. Thin lines delicately repeat the red in the mirror frame, which has a black and red inner moulding. A string of amber beads hangs on the wall, and repeats the shimmer of the bright brass candelabra which hangs aloft, and which is drawn carefully enough for a craftsman to reproduce.

Pattern-Pictures[272]

Both designer and painter may find abundant suggestion in this picture, which, with Ver Meer's "Lady at the Spinet," I should describe as *pattern-pictures*—that is to say, while they are thoroughly painter's pictures, and give all the peculiar qualities of oil-painting in the rendering of tone and values, they yet show in their colour scheme the decorative quality, and might be translated into patterns of the same proportions and keys of colours.

As examples of what might be termed picture-patterns we might recur to the wall paintings, as I have said, of ancient Egypt and early art generally, for their simplest forms; but to take a much later instance, and from the art of Florence in the fifteenth century, look at Botticelli's charming little picture of "The Nativity," in the National Gallery. It has all the intentional, or perhaps instinctive, ornamental aim of Italian art, and its colour scheme shows a most dainty and delicate invention in the strictest relation to the subject and sentiment, and is arranged with the utmost subtlety and the nicest art.

Botticelli

The ring of angels above, for instance, is partly relieved upon a gilded ground—to represent the dome of heaven. They bear olive branches, and the colour of their robes alternates in the following order: rose, olive (shot with gold), and white.

The *rose-coloured* angels have *olive and white wings*; the *white angels, rose and olive wings*; and *the olive angels, white and rose wings.*

This part of the picture by itself forms a most beautiful pattern motive, while it expresses the idea of peace and goodwill.

Then on the brown and gold thatch of the [273]stable occur three more angels in white, rose, and green, respectively. Against a pale sky rise rich olive-green trees, forming the background.

The Virgin strikes the brightest ray of colour [274]in red under-robe and sky-blue mantle. There is a gray white ass and a pale brown cow behind her.

St. Joseph is in steel gray with a golden orange mantle over.

The brightest white occurs in the drapery upon which the infant Christ lies.

An angel with a group of men appears, kneeling on the left relieved against white rocks; their colours are—the angel's wings—peacock blue and green, and a pale rose robe. The next figure is in scarlet; the next yellow; and the third man wears pale rose over rich grass-green.

Of the shepherds on the right the first one is in russet and white, the next steely gray, and the angel is in white with rose and pale green wings.

The ground is generally warm white and brown, with dark olive-coloured grass and foliage, so that the pattern of the picture is mainly a ground of olive, gold, and white, relieved by spots of rose, white, blue, yellow, and rose-red and scarlet—the colour in the groups of angels embracing men in front being the deepest in tone.

The first angel in this group (on the left) wears green shot with gold, with shot green and gold wings, the human being in dark olive and rich crimson red.

Next is a white angel with pale rose wings; the man in gray with a red mantle over.

Last is an angel in rose, with rose and red wings, the man being in scarlet with gray mantle over. All the men hold olive branches, and the group emphatically illustrates the idea of "on earth peace and goodwill towards men," thus [275]ending on the keynote both of colour and idea given in the ring of angels above.

Thus it is not only a lovely picture, but an exquisite pattern.

Holbein

Another instance of a picture-pattern extremely strong and brilliant in its realization of the full force and value of bright colour opposed by the strongest black and white, may be found in Holbein's splendid "Ambassadors," also in our National Collection.

Botticelli

The circular picture of the Madonna and Child, with St. John and an angel, by Botticelli, is also [276]another beautiful instance of pictorial pattern, and of design well adapted and adequately filling its space, while full of delicate draughtsmanship, poetic sentiment, and extremely ornate in its colour.

Carlo Crivelli

Still more strictly ornamental in character and aim is Carlo Crivelli's "Annunciation." Amazingly [277]rich in invention, and beautifully designed detail, and magnificently decorative in its colour scheme of brick reds and whites, and pale pinks and steel grays, and yellows, varied with scarlet [278]and black, green, blue and gold, in the costumes and draperies, sparkling with jewels, and brightened with rays and patterns of gold.

Perugino

Hardly less ornamental in its more conscious grace and Renaissance feeling is Perugino's triptych of the Virgin adoring, with St. Michael on one wing and St. Raphael and Tobias on the other. It is a splendid deep-toned harmony of blues, and warm flesh tones and golden hair, varied by opals, rose red, bronze, green, white, and purple and orange.

Titian

Titian's "Bacchus and Ariadne" is, perhaps, more what I have described as a pattern-picture, and is of a much later type. The full flush of colour and pagan joy of the Renaissance is here paramount, expressed with the masterly freedom of drawing and magnificent colour sense of the great [279]Venetian master. Yet, looking through the life, the movement, the swing and vitality of the figures, and the power and poetry by which the story is conveyed, we shall find a fine ornate design, sustaining an extremely rich and sumptuous pattern of colour. We have a spread of deep-toned blue sky barred with silvery white and gray clouds, great masses of brown and green foliage swaying against it, above a band of deep blue sea, and a field of rich golden brown earth. Warm flesh tones, deep and pale, break upon this with a gorgeous pattern of flying rose, blue, scarlet, orange, and white draperies, varied with the spotted coats of the leopards, the black of the dog, and the copper vessel and warm white of tumbled drapery.

[280]Keats might have had this picture in his mind when he wrote the song in "Endymion":

"And as I sat, over the light blue hillsThere came a noise of revellers: the rillsInto the wide stream came of purple hue.'Twas Bacchus and his crew!

"The earnest trumpet speaks, and silver thrillsFrom kissing cymbals made a merry din—'Twas Bacchus and his kin!

"Like to a moving vintage down they came,Crowned with green leaves, and faces all on flame;All madly dancing through the pleasant valley,To scare thee, Melancholy!"

The "Sacred and Profane Love" of the same painter, in the Borghese Gallery at Rome, is an even more splendid example of colour and tone, and is probably the finest of all Titian's works.

Paul Veronese

In Paul Veronese we find a cooler key of colour generally, with a fondness for compositions of figures with classical architecture, the rich patterned robes and varied heads contrasting pleasantly with the severe verticals and smooth surfaces of the marble columns—a sumptuous and dignified kind of picture-pattern, and fully adapted to the decoration of Venetian churches and palaces of the Renaissance.

F. Madox Brown

Madox Brown's "Christ washing St. Peter's Feet," now in the Tate Gallery, is a modern picture-pattern, and an extremely fine one.

These are but a few instances out of many, and the subject of colour and pattern, like the expression of line and form, of which it is a part, is so large and its sides so multitudinous that to deal with the subject fully and illustrate it adequately [281]would need, not ten chapters, but ten hundred, and could only be compassed by the history of art itself.

Conclusion

If anything I have said on the subject, or have been able to show by way of illustration, has served in any way to clear away obscurities, or to lighten the labours of students, or to suggest fresh ideas to the minds of any of my readers in the theory, history, or practice of art, I shall feel that my work has not been in vain, and, at all events, I can only say that I have endeavoured to give here the results of my own thoughts and experience in art.

[282]Some may look upon art as a means of livelihood only, a handmaid of commerce, or as a branch of knowledge, to be acquired only so far as to enable one to impart it to others; others may regard it as a polite amusement; others, again, as an absorbing pursuit and passion, demanding the closest devotion: but from whatever point of view we may regard it, do not let us forget that the pursuit of beauty in art offers the best of educations for the faculties, that its interest continually increases, and its pleasures and successes are the most refined and satisfying.

Printed in the USA
CPSIA information can be obtained
at www.ICGtesting.com
LVHW010107080324
773896LV00036B/1481